Simon Grave
and the
School of
Casual Invisibility

Len Boswell

www.blackrosewriting.com

Black Rose Writing | Texas

First printing

This is a work of fiction. Names, characters, businesses, places, events, and incidents are either the products of the author's imagination or used in a fictitious manner. Any resemblance to actual persons, living or dead, or actual events is purely coincidental.

ISBN: 978-1-68433-875-7
PUBLISHED BY BLACK ROSE WRITING
www.blackrosewriting.com

Printed in the United States of America
Suggested Retail Price (SRP) $18.95

Simon Grave and the School of Casual Invisibility is printed in Palatino Linotype

*As a planet-friendly publisher, Black Rose Writing does its best to eliminate unnecessary waste to reduce paper usage and energy costs, while never compromising the reading experience. As a result, the final word count vs. page count may not meet common expectations.

To all I love without condition,
To all I love without omission.

Never doubt.

Other books by Len Boswell

Simon Grave Mysteries:
A Grave Misunderstanding
Simon Grave and the Curious Incident of the Cat in the Daytime
Simon Grave and the Drone of the Basque Orvilles
Simon Grave and the Sons of Irony

Other Mysteries:
Flicker: A Paranormal Mystery
Skeleton: A Bare Bones Mystery

Memoirs:
Santa Takes a Tumble
Unboxing Raymond

Nonfiction:
The Leadership Secrets of Squirrels
Stick Figures: The Life and Art of Len Boswell

Fantasies:
The Cave of the Six Arrows

Simon Grave

and the
School of Casual
Invisibility

The problem with invisibility remains to be seen.

1

Jeremy Polk, Crab Cove's diminutive medical examiner looked down at nothing, and seeing nothing, looked up into the face of the Class 7 simdroid officer, who towered over him. "What is this, some kind of joke?"

The simdroid, Officer Larry, one of many Officer Larrys on the force, all dead ringers for the long-dead actor Morgan Freeman, intoned what he thought would be a satisfactory reply, one selected from his database of sonorous utterances. "Not everything seen is visible."

Polk pulled himself erect, back arched, chin high in a way that had earned him the nickname Little Napoleon. "So it *is* a joke. Who put you up to this? Captain Morgan? Grave?"

Officer Larry pointed down at the nothing. "It's a body, sir, and quite dead. A woman, I would think from the indentation in the grass."

Polk squinted at the grass. There was an indentation and an outline that could only be a woman. She seemed to be lying on her side, one arm raised as if she knew the answer to an important question. "Humph."

"The man over there by the gazebo hailed me. He was walking his dog and tripped over it—I mean, her."

Polk looked over at the man, who returned a little wave in recognition. "An invisible body?"

"Yes, sir."

"Well, we'll see about that." Polk knelt beside the indentation and tried to touch the grass, but his hand came to rest in midair, a good ten inches from the ground, startling him. "Holy—"

"Yes," said Officer Larry, "I think you'll find that was her hip. If you continue up and down the length of her, you'll find that she was quite trim and fit."

Polk had examined hundreds of bodies in his career, but somehow, touching this invisible body seemed a violation of her privacy, almost ghoulish. "Later, perhaps."

He looked around the scene. The body was resting on the grass just off one of six gravel paths that crisscrossed the town square, a grassy park a block square, bounded by Main Street to the west, Imperial Avenue to the east, Blue Crab Boulevard to the north, and Shell Street to the south. All the paths converged on the gazebo at the center of the square and the circular path around it. The path there was wider, allowing space enough for seated viewing of town events and concerts at the benches that lined its entire circumference, as well as a single "chess" station, a small granite table scored with a chessboard. The two small stools around it were now occupied by two men in deep thought over the array of their chess pieces. "Okay, let's cordon off the entire square. And get statements from the dog guy and the two chess players."

"Shall I call Captain Morgan?"

The words startled Polk. "Wait, what, you haven't called this in?"

Officer Larry looked down at the ground. "I thought you should be the first to see this, sir."

Polk sighed. "All right, all right, get to work. I'll give Morgan a call."

Officer Larry nodded and shuffled away toward the dog man.

Polk looked down at the indentation in the grass. "We'll sort this out for you, dear. Rest easy, help is on the way."

He motioned to his personal drone, a new Apple 84 named Toetag, and no bigger than a teacup. He was still getting used to the idea of a personal drone and often found himself reaching for the cellphone that the drone had replaced. "Get on the horn. We need Morgan and at least a dozen officers. Stat."

Toetag waggled in the air, then shot straight up, stopping a hundred feet above the ground, where he knew the reception would be strong and clear.

Captain Morgan's personal drone, Rum, picked up on the second ring. "You have reached Captain Morgan. Rum here."

Toetag could imagine Rum hovering over the captain's desk, dressed all up like a pirate and brandishing his cutlass. "Hello, Rum, this is Toetag for medical examiner Jeremy Polk."

"Hello, Toetag, long time no see. How may I be of help?"

"I need to speak with Captain Morgan on an urgent matter."

"Hmm, well I'm afraid the cap'n is in deep thought."

Toetag could hear a noise in the background. "Is that snoring I hear?"

"Um, yes, the cap'n gets his *deepest* thoughts while he's asleep."

"Well, you need to wake him up. We've a kind of situation here at the town square."

"Oh, what kind of situation?"

"We've discovered an invisible body."

Rum went silent for some seconds. "Is this a joke?"

2

Detective Simon Grave was trying his best not to doze off as his father's fiancé, Ida Notion, droned on and on about the wedding plans.

"I'm thinking we'll stick with red roses all the way. No need to confuse things with this flower and that. Keep it simple, you know? But elegant. Right, Jacob?"

Simon's father, Jacob Grave, now just a short shuffling walk from his mid-seventies, snorted his way back into consciousness long enough to say, "Whatever you think, dear. Roses it is."

Ida frowned at him. "You were asleep, weren't you?"

"Of course not." He tried his best to sit up straighter in his recliner, but it was clearly a struggle. To Simon, he seemed to be growing weaker by the day. He had grown thin where he should have been plump, and soft where he should have been firm. Sleep seemed to be his default setting, and his skin had grown almost translucent, revealing blue vein highways heading everywhere and nowhere. The question, at least to Simon, was whether the next ceremony would be a wedding to the tiny gypsy psychic or a funeral, and funeral seemed to have an edge.

"Need some help?" said Simon, standing up and moving to the recliner, trying his best not to wince from the pain shooting through both knees. Now well into his forties, he was beginning to experience the beginning of the ultimate slide to eventual oblivion. But he still had

4

his thick black hair, his square-jawed good looks, and the grayish-blue eyes that made him, well, almost handsome.

Jacob tried again to straighten himself, but failed. "I guess. Just help me find the damned handle to this contraption."

Simon bent down, grabbed the handle, and tugged the recliner back into a straight-up position, nearly launching Jacob into the air.

Jacob startled, grabbing onto the arm rests. "Easy, son. This isn't a damned catapult."

Simon grabbed him by the shoulders and pulled him up to a sitting position.

Ida seemed unfazed by Operation Recliner. "Anyway, there's the matter of the reception to think about. What do you think about a wedding singer, Jacob? I've got tapes here from sixteen possibilities. Ten men and six women, but I think the singer should be a man, don't you? I mean, it's more traditional and—"

Ida suddenly stopped, her face growing pale. "Oh, sweet Jesus!"

Simon had seen this look before, the look that came over her when she was having one of her psychic visions. "What, Ida?"

"Someone's been murdered, but I can't see who. It's very strange. All I see is grass."

"That's it? Grass?"

"Yes, and an overwhelming feeling of dread and violence." She shuddered. "It's awful."

Simon's personal drone, Barry, who had been hovering silently in the corner of the room with Jacob's and Ida's personal drones, Buddy and Crystal Ball, suddenly began to waggle in the air. "You have a call, sir."

"Put it on speaker."

"Okay, sir. Here's Rum."

After a short pause, Rum began. "This is Rum for Captain Morgan. He requests your immediate presence at the town square. We have a situation where your skills and experience are needed for a satisfactory conclusion."

"What kind of situation?"

"We've discovered an invisible dead body."

Simon rolled his eyes. "Wait, is this some kind of joke?"

3

Grave arrived at the town square with his usual fanfare, the sound of gospel music blasting from the radio of his antique Austin Healey Sprite. The radio was stuck on that station, at full volume, a situation that Grave now welcomed. It may have annoyed if not deafened everyone else, but it helped him think.

And what he was thinking now was that he hoped the body was not Rippley Blunt, the daughter of his partner, Sergeant Barry Blunt, a man so nondescript he was almost invisible. The man was cloudlike, as was his wife, June Thursday, so it was not wholly unexpected that their offspring would be equally cloudlike, or in fact, invisible, which she surely was.

Grave's hope rested on the fact that he knew there was more than one invisible person in Crab Cove and the Greater Crabopolis. In fact, there were many, all thanks to Rippley Blunt. She had been born invisible, but had quickly figured out how to make herself visible or invisible at will. In no time, she had shown her parents how they, too, could control their visibility, like a lightbulb controlled by a rheostat, the light going from bright to dim with a simple twist of the dial. The training had gone so well, in fact, that she decided to teach her playmates how to become invisible at will. And from there, it was just days before she decided to open the Rippley Blunt School of Casual Invisibility, welcoming students of all backgrounds and ages. Her mother had suggested the name, but with *causal* instead of *casual*. Rippley had accidently flipped the letters, and the name had stuck.

Grave pulled into the nearest parking spot along Main Street and turned off the electric motor, the abruptly ended gospel music briefly echoing through the square. He could see Polk and Morgan standing in the grass along one of the paths, one a man so small he needed a box to reach the examination table, the other an overweight, bald blockhead of a man. A dozen or more simdroid officers were running around them with crime tape, trying to secure the square.

Morgan removed his hands from his ears and motioned Grave to join them. "Over here."

Grave, a tall, Dudley Do-Right of a man, extricated himself from the little car and jogged up to them, forgoing any greetings. "Is it her, um, Rippley?"

Captain Morgan grabbed Grave by the shoulders. "Oh, no, no, no. It's a young woman, not a child. I thought Rum told you that." He glared back at Rum, who was hovering near his shoulder. "But apparently not."

Grave looked around. "Where is the body?"

"Right there," said Polk, pointing at a spot a few feet away from them.

Grave squinted at the spot. "Invisible, all right." He turned back to Polk. "What do we know?"

"Not much," said Polk. "I've scanned her already, so the basics are that she's probably in her early twenties and has a broken neck."

"Broken neck?"

"Severely broken, head twisted backwards. Looks like the work of someone who's had military training or martial arts."

"What about time of death?"

"I would say last night, between nine and ten or thereabouts."

Friday night on the town square, thought Grave. The streets and the square would have been jumping, people everywhere, on sidewalks, in restaurants, or just strolling around the square. "What about witnesses?"

Morgan shook his head. "How could there be witnesses? She's invisible. All we know is a man walking his dog tripped over her this morning."

Grave stroked his chin. "Well, maybe she was and maybe she wasn't"

"What do you mean?"

"You know, like when the werewolf is killed, he always turns back into his human form."

Morgan scoffed. "We're not dealing with werewolves, and besides, she's done it kind of backwards, going from a human to a werewolf, albeit an invisible one."

"Stop it, the two of you," said Polk. "We clearly have two possibilities for her and two possibilities for her killer. Either they were both invisible, in which case we will have no witnesses. Or one of them was visible, in which case we should have witnesses who saw a man or a woman seemingly wrestling with the air."

Grave nodded. "That makes logical sense, to a point, but if she were invisible to begin with, how would the killer even find her? I mean, we can't see her. How could he?"

"Maybe," said Polk, "maybe an invisible man can see an invisible woman."

"Which would mean," said Morgan, "our killer may have also been a student at Rippley's school."

"Exactly," said Polk. "We just have to identify them."

"Maybe," said Morgan, "but first things first." He pointed at one of the lampposts along the street. "This place is covered by a shitload of CCTV cameras. I'll get someone to collect the tapes, so we can view them back at the station. And we'll need to talk to the business owners around the square; see if they saw anything, or could possibly identify the woman."

"Well," said Polk, "as I've said, no one is going to identify an invisible woman."

Grave nodded. "We'll have to get Blunt and Rippley involved. The woman must have been one of her students. And the man as well, as you say, Polk."

"Exactly my thought," said Morgan. "Let's head over there now, Grave."

"All right."

"Wait, what about the body?" said Polk. "Can I take her to the morgue?"

Morgan scratched his head. "I don't see why not."

"Okay, I'll see to it."

Morgan suddenly had a thought. "Wait, what about her belongings? A purse? Her drone?"

Polk nodded. "Um, nothing sir."

"Maybe the killer took them, or maybe someone else stole them after the fact."

Morgan grunted. "Maybe. Perhaps the videos will help us there."

"Okay," said Grave. "I'll follow you to Blunt's house."

Morgan shook his head. "Wait a minute, Grave. I need to talk to you about another matter. Leave your car and its damned gospel music here, and come along with me."

"Another matter?"

Morgan chuckled. "Don't worry, nothing serious. Come on, let's go."

4

June Thursday, ever cloudlike, sat opposite the new applicant to Rippley Blunt's School of Casual Invisibility, an empty chair beside her.

"Will Rippley be joining us?" said the young man. Actually, he was more teenager than man, despite the fact that his application clearly read "Age 23." He was tall and gangly, with a half shaved head that was all the rage now, in 2054. The other half was a blonde wave that obscured his left eye. She had the feeling that she was talking to a young cyclops.

"Yes," she said, "but first I'd like to review your application."

"Of course," he said, brushing his hair away from his eye.

Well, he does have two eyes, thought June. "Now, I'm a little confused by your answer to question twelve."

"Oh? Which one is that?"

"Your reason for wanting to be casually invisible."

"Oh, that one. What's the problem?"

"You say, 'for my personal security,' and that's it. Can you expand on that?"

He sighed. "Okay, it's like this. I have a bad gambling addiction. I owe people all over town, so . . ."

"So you want to avoid paying back your debts."

He shook his head vigorously. "Oh, no, I've been paying them back. It's just that there's this one guy who's been threatening me to pay up on—what can I call it?—an *unreasonable* timetable."

"He's threatened you with physical harm?"

"Worse," he said, his lips trembling. *"Death."*

June sat back in her seat for some seconds, then leaned forward. "Look, I'll make a deal with you."

"A deal?"

"Yes, I'll admit you to the school on the condition that you seek help for your addiction."

He puffed out his cheeks, and shook his head. "I've tried that before, and it didn't work."

"Well, I'm afraid that condition is *firm*. You'll have to find a new therapist and try again. Otherwise, I'm afraid I can't admit you."

He nodded. "Okay, okay, whatever you say. Just admit me. *Please*."

"Well, as you know, there's one last thing."

"Yes, the reciting of the Laws of Invisibility, from memory."

"All right, can you do it?"

He nodded vigorously.

"Go on, then."

He cleared his throat and began:

"Law One: Invisibility will be used only for good.

"Law Two: Invisibility will never be used to harm, deceive, or embarrass.

"Law Three: Invisibility will never be used for lude or immoral purposes.

"Law Four: Invisibility will never be taught to others."

June smiled at him. "Perfect."

He smiled back, then raised a hand. "May I ask a question?"

"Of course."

"Why do you need that last one, Law Four? It sounds like you're trying to avoid competition." When June began to frown, he quickly added, "I mean, not that I would break that law, mind."

"Good, good. In our early days, we only had the first three laws, but we found that people were teaching others the skill without supporting the first three laws. For example, teenage boys using their invisibility to spy on the girls volley ball team in their locker room."

He chuckled, then quickly composed himself, trying his best to look serious. "I see, I see. Good point."

June nodded. "All right, then." She extended her hand across the desk. "Welcome to Rippley's school."

He beamed. "Thank you, thank you. Now, can I meet Rippley?"

Now it was June's turn to chuckle. "Why, yes. In fact, she's been here the whole time."

Then came a giggle that could only have come from a little girl.

The boy looked around. "Is that her?"

June nodded and turned in the direction of the chair next to her. A cloud began to form, then the outline of a little girl, and then the girl herself, completely visible and beaming at her new student. She had red hair and freckles and a disarming smile. His first thought was *Pippi Longstocking.*

"Welcome to my school," she said, extending her little hand.

Morgan got right to the point. "I have some decisions to make, *big* decisions."

The words did not surprise Grave, who had noticed a change in Captain Morgan over the past several months. The man's constant but never-acted-upon musings of retirement had now become something more definite. And pressure from the new mayor, Lester "Les" Change, the first simdroid elected to public office and a dead-on replica of President Ronald Reagan, wasn't helping. Change wanted change, particularly in the roles of simdroids in the Crab Cove Police Department.

Grave got right to the point. "So you're going to retire?"

Morgan was taken aback. "You knew?"

Grave nodded. "You haven't been yourself. We've all noticed it."

Morgan slumped back in the seat of the driverless police cruiser and looked out the window. "The town's changing. The land's shrinking, the population's growing, and—let's face it—I'm no longer the man for this job."

"Nonsense, sir. If I may say, the only change I see around here is Les Change. We just have to figure out how to deal with him and his demands."

Morgan shook his head. "I appreciate that, Grave, I really do, but I'm afraid matters have taken a turn for the worse. He's asked for my resignation, by the end of the month."

"Resignation? Why?"

Morgan sighed. "I refused a direct order."

"On what?"

"It doesn't matter what. The man—the droid—is just insufferable."

Grave nodded. "Yes, sir. So, you were talking about decisions that needed to be made."

Morgan chuckled sardonically. "Decisions, decisions, *big* decisions, the first being succession."

"Your replacement."

"Yes. The mayor wanted to make the decision himself, but the town council, bless them, said no. They want to form a special search committee, to interview candidates and make a recommendation to the full council."

Grave nodded. "Sounds right."

"Yes, the council has been fair, at least about the search committee. The council will appoint three members of the committee, Mayor Change will appoint another, and I will have the option of adding the final member."

Grave hoped he wasn't talking about him. "Um."

"I will also have the right to nominate a candidate for the Captaincy and to appoint an acting chief."

Grave wasn't sure where the Captain was going with this. "Sir, that seems eminently fair, but—"

Morgan chuckled. "And I want you to be acting chief."

Grave flushed. He felt light-headed. "Sir, I'm not cut out for your job. I'm just—"

"Stop, stop right there. Don't say another word. Think about it. You're the best damned detective I have."

"But sir—"

"And the only one who can stand up to Les Change."

Now it was Grave's turn to slump back into his seat. "How long would I have to do that, this acting thing?"

The council would like to make a decision in six weeks, and they want the acting chief to begin immediately. I'm to stand down. Administrative leave."

"Immediately? Now I know how convicted felons feel facing their jail sentences. I don't know if I can make it that long."

Morgan laughed and slapped Grave on the knee. "You'll do fine, I know it. Now, as to the other decisions, I'm going to nominate Detective Snoot to the search committee, which will take all her time. That leaves her partner, Detective Loblolly, in need of a temporary partner."

"I see. Well, there are a couple of simdroids that have shown promise, sir."

"Patrolmen?"

"Yes, one or two of the Larrys."

"No, no, I have something else in mind. I want you to take her on."

Grave looked confused. "I thought I was acting chief? That would leave Sergeant Blunt without a partner. So why not a Blunt-Loblolly team?"

"No, I'm putting Blunt on a desk for the duration of this damned invisibility case. With his daughter in the mix, he needs to recuse himself from the investigation."

"So I will be acting chief *and* lead detective?"

Morgan gave Grave an impish smile. "Yes, and it will give you a chance to know her better."

"Polly? I mean, Detective Loblolly?"

"Oh, Grave. Grave, Grave, Grave, a blind man could see there's something going on between you two."

"Sir, I—"

Morgan hushed him. "Now don't say another word. And look, we're here."

The hovercruiser slowed to a stop, but Grave's heart was racing.

Sergeant Barry Blunt's cloudy smile of greeting vanished altogether when Captain Morgan explained the reason for their visit on Blunt's cherished day off.

"That's terrible, captain. Rippley will be devastated."

"We'll leave the telling to you, when you think the time is appropriate—but soon, Blunt, soon."

Grave put his hand on Blunt's shoulder. "Right now, we need to talk with you and June, get a feeling for the school and her students."

"Right, right. I won't be of much help. June handles the administrative side of things. Best start with her. Come on, follow me."

Blunt led them down a long hallway to what used to be their Great Room, but was now clearly a classroom. Charts and graphs lined the walls, along with large blowups of Rippley in various stages of invisibility, from there to not there. A group of about a dozen students, mostly children, stood in a circle at the center of the room, little Rippley, three years old going on thirty-five, at its center, her voice light and friendly, but barely audible.

Barry stopped them at the doorway. "Wait here. I'll get June." He walked away from them to a corner of the room, where a cloud known as June Thursday sat behind a large official-looking desk. As cloudlike as she was, it was clear that she was shaken by what Barry was whispering in her ear. She immediately stood and walked with Barry back to the door.

"Captain, Grave," she said. "What in the world?"

"Yes," said Grave. "It's awful."

"Terrible," said Morgan.

"She's going to be very upset," said June. "Whoever it is. She loves her students, even the ones that don't quite get it, like Bill Jackson over there." She pointed in the direction of a man who was visible only from the neck down. "That's the best he can do, and it scares the bejesus out of his family. Can you imagine running into him on the street?" She attempted a laugh, but failed.

Captain Morgan touched her arm. "Is there somewhere else we can talk?"

June nodded and pointed them back down the hall. "The living room." She walked past them and headed down the hall.

Morgan grabbed Grave by the arm and whispered, "You take the lead, Grave. Consider this the start of your tenure as acting chief."

Grave gulped. "Yes, sir."

They followed June and Blunt to the living room and sat down on a couch opposite them.

Grave cleared his throat. "The first thing is knowing who the victim was. We know she was young, and that's about it. Oh, and that she was invisible when we found her."

June nodded. "I'd say there's a good chance she was invisible just before she was killed. We have no experience with death in that respect, but we do know that going from completely invisible to visible doesn't happen with the snap of your fingers. The change is usually quite intentional and takes time to click in. Rippley says it's like trying to deal with a tricky zipper. It takes time to align things just right. So, did she die quickly?"

"Her neck was snapped," said Grave.

June shuddered. "Quickly, then. So I'd say she was definitely invisible at the time."

"And that raises the question, why?"

June's eyes went wide. "Oh, my god. That could also mean she was killed by someone invisible."

"Another of your students, perhaps."

"Maybe," said June. "We've had some trouble with our graduates teaching the skill to others."

"Do you know who those students are?"

"Some of them."

"Do you have a list of current and former students?"

June nodded. "Better than that, we have a folder on each one of them: their applications, contact information, and photographs in every stage of invisibility they could manage. Oh, and also the reason they applied to the school."

"Why they wanted to be invisible, you mean?"

"Yes, we try to be careful not to teach bank robbers and the like."

Grave chuckled. "Sounds like a good idea." He turned to Blunt. "I'm sorry to end your day off, but if you could collect those applications and bring them back to the station that would be great."

Blunt sighed. "All right, no problem."

He began to stand, but June grabbed him by the arm. "Wait, honey." She turned to Grave. "I interviewed all those people and know things about them that aren't on the forms. I can lend a hand."

A tiny voice interrupted them. "And so can I," said Rippley, wiping away a tear as she became visible.

"Oh, honey," said June. "You heard? Everything?"

Rippley gave a quick nod and sniffed back tears. "Everything. Do we know who it is?"

"No," said Grave, "but perhaps with your help, we can find out. We're going to go through all the folders and hopefully find her."

"I'd like to see her," said Rippley.

June grabbed her and pulled her close. "Oh, no, honey, you don't want to do that."

"Yes, yes I do. I may be able to make her visible."

Grave smiled. "You can do that?"

"I think so. When my students get stuck on invisible, I can sometimes shake them loose. Lay my hands on them. Sometimes it works and sometimes we just have to wait it out. Anyway, worth a try. Where is she?"

"At the morgue," said Grave. "We'll take you there."

"I'm coming, too," said June. "I want to be with my baby."

Grave nodded. "Fine, you can ride with Captain Morgan and me." He turned to Sergeant Blunt. "But I need you to gather up the folders and take them to the station. We won't be long, and we'll join you there."

Blunt was about to object, but Captain Morgan gave him his brow-raising, you-better-comply look. "Very well."

He bent down and held Rippley by the shoulders. "Are you going to be all right?"

She nodded and gave him a weak smile. "Yes, daddy."

He stood and turned to Grave. "See you at the station."

The driverless police hovercruiser did its thing, accelerating away from Blunt's house, the scenery almost a blur as it picked up speed.

Rippley giggled. "It's fast, isn't it? It tickles my tummy."

"Would you like us to slow down?" said Grave.

"No, *faster*, please."

Grave hated driverless vehicles. Statistics said they were perfectly safe, but Grave always cringed at intersections, expecting horrific collisions. Even so, he pressed a button on the rear console and issued the command. "Faster."

The hovercruiser lurched forward, all of them holding onto their seats as the whine of the engine became more like the shriek of a banshee.

"Oh, my," said Rippley. "Oh, my."

Grave tried not to look out the window. "This will only take a few minutes now. So, Rippley, the captain and I know very little about invisibility. Can you explain the process?"

Rippley seemed to struggle with the word. "Process?"

"You know, how you get your students to go from visible to invisible."

"Oh, that. Well, have you ever heard of auras?"

Grave remembered reading something about them. "You mean, like some kind of glow around certain people. Different colors, and not everyone can see them."

"Yes, but there's more. Have you ever seen one of those old-timey paintings with people standing around with halos over their heads?"

"Yes, of course."

"Well, those are really auras, and they're as old as time. You have a very nice aura, if I may say so."

"Me?"

"Yes, and at the moment, it's blue."

"Blue? As opposed to what?"

"Different colors—red, orange, yellow, green, indigo, violet—each supposedly with a different meaning, each a different layer of your aura."

"What does blue mean?"

"To some it would mean you're intuitive, spiritual, and a freethinker, but that's just mumbo-jumbo created by people who don't really understand auras."

"So what are they?"

Rippley cocked her head. "I'm still learning, but to put it most simply, they're energy fields. They surround our bodies, and they can be manipulated."

"To make us visible or invisible?"

"And everything in between. To be fully invisible, I activate each layer and drop them down, like a shade. To be visible, I pull them up to my head and in."

Grave had no response to that other than, "Humph."

"I have a theory," said Rippley, "if you'd like to hear it."

They all nodded, even June.

"I think there was a time when the entire human race was invisible, a way to avoid large predators and move freely across the globe."

"And now?" said Grave.

"Over time, our auras grew weaker, making more of us visible. I think some of the phenomena we think of as ghosts are just throwbacks, regular people who're invisible."

Grave frowned. He wondered how his ghost friend Victoria would feel about this. "Ghosts?"

"It's just a theory," said Rippley. "I could be dead wrong about that. But to get to my point, my parents themselves are throwbacks of a sort; their natural state is partial invisibility."

"Indeed," said Grave. "So, if I'm hearing you correctly, you being the offspring of two throwbacks—no offense, June—by some genetic magic, you were born *completely* invisible. That's your natural state."

"Yes, I'm the ultimate throwback, and I was upset not to be like my parents. It's not fun being the only invisible person in the world, ghosts notwithstanding."

"I bet," said Grave. He sensed the slowing of the hovercruiser. They were almost there. "So somehow, now you've figured out how to make yourself visible."

"Exactly, I learned how to manipulate my aura, changing the energy field at will. I can even strobe."

They all startled as Rippley went from there to not there, strobing on and off at great speed.

"Wow," said Grave.

"Wow," said Morgan.

"Wow," said June.

"We have arrived, please exit carefully," said the hovercruiser. "And thank you for traveling with me today through the wonderful city of Crab Cove and the Greater Crabopolis. This message brought to you by Mayor Lester Change."

Grave groaned, and Morgan grumbled.

8

Sergeant Barry Blunt huffed and puffed his way up the steps to the station door, trailed by his personal drone, Object. After struggling to open the door and waiving Object in, he walked to his desk and dropped the heavy box of student folders on top of it. Several simdroid Larrys stopped and looked at him briefly, then went about their business. "Where is everybody?"

One of the Larrys stopped his examination of a knife long enough to say in the voice of Morgan Freeman, "They're all in the conference room."

"Come on, Object." He picked up the box, carted it to the conference room, and dropped it on the table. Detectives Snoot, Loblolly, Holmes, and Smithers-Watson paid no attention. They were sorting through a pile of what looked like a hundred or more CCTV tapes. Loblolly's drone, Pine Cone, hovered in a corner of the room with Snoot's new drone, Midnight, a state-of-the-art Ramrod Midnight Special 437XL, which had the amazing ability to scramble itself into a swarm of smaller, bee-sized drones capable of independent or synchronized flight.

Over the past several years, he, Grave, and the other four had formed a smooth-working team, each bringing unique skills to the table. Detective Polly Loblolly, a knockout blonde, was the newest to the team, joining the force just months ago after her previous workplace in Delaware found itself under water, the entire state sunk under the

Atlantic, another victim of global warming. Detective Amanda Snoot was Loblolly's polar opposite. Rail thin, with a frown seemingly frozen on her face, she was nevertheless a gifted detective—and fearless.

And prone to interrupting anyone's thoughts. "I don't suppose you could give us a hand?" she said. "We're trying to decide which tapes to view first. You know, from that invisible body thingy."

"Well," said Blunt, "I was hoping you would give me some help with the student data from my daughter's School of Casual Invisibility. We need to sort them by age and gender for starters."

"Ah," said Loblolly. "Our potential suspects."

"And the potential victim as well."

"Wait," said Snoot. "We don't know who the victim was?"

"Not yet. Grave, Morgan, June, and Rippley are on their way to the morgue to see if Rippley can make the body visible. If not, we'll have to find her in these student folders."

Charlize Holmes, a simdroid designed to look like the young Charlize Theron but with the mannerisms and skills of Sherlock Holmes, even to the point of wearing his Inverness cape and Deerstalker hat, seemed not to hear the discussion about the folders. "Look, I have an idea about the tapes. Rather than view them one by one, let's sync them by time and location, and play the whole scene out on our Surround Vision system. We'll have a virtual 3-D crime scene. We can walk around in it and perhaps find our killer."

"What a wonderful idea," said Smithers-Watson, her simdroid companion, who looked like the young Peter O'Toole, but with the deep voice of Richard Burton. He had begun his career as a butler in the Hawthorne Mansion, but had since been reprogrammed to serve as Charlize Holmes's boon companion, Dr. Smithers-Watson. As per his role, he wore a black Haversack jacket with shoulder and elbow pads to simulate the good doctor's favorite attire.

"Elementary," said Charlize. "Now, Watson, I need you to help me cart these down to the tech lab, so the technicians can create the Surround Vision tape."

"Right, right," said Smithers-Watson, gathering up the tapes and putting them in a large box.

Charlize turned to Blunt. "I see you brought the student folders. Good, that's the first thing I thought of when I heard the victim was from Rippley's school. I think we'll find her there, along with her killer or killers."

"Killers?" said Blunt, taken aback.

"Just a thought. Students run in packs, and there is often more intrigue in a classroom than in the wider world."

Blunt shrugged. "If you say so."

"I do, indeed. Now, Watson, are we ready to go?"

"Yes," said Smithers-Watson, lifting the box of tapes.

Charlize turned to the others. "Right, well, we'll be on our way." She looked at Blunt. "I'd sort them by age and gender first, if I were you."

Blunt shook his head. She could be such a pain at times. "Of course, of course, and perhaps we'll have our victim and our killer by the time you get back."

Charlize frowned. "Oh, I doubt that, but I do appreciate your confidence."

Without another word, Charlize and Smithers-Watson walked past them and out of the room.

Blunt puffed out his cheeks. "She can be insufferable at times."

"You can say that again," said Snoot.

"She can be—"

"Stop," said Loblolly. "Let's get to work. Here, put the women and girls on the left and the men and boys on the right."

They all began digging into the box of folders, extracting one at a time, flipping each open to determine the sex of the student, and placing it in the appropriate pile.

Snoot laughed when she opened her first folder. "Oh, shit, listen to this. The student's name is *Ann Aesthesia*."

Blunt chuckled. "I know, I know. We could barely contain ourselves when she applied."

"Do you think it's her real name?"

"Yes, we check IDs."

"Wow."

"Why do parents do that to their children?" said Loblolly.

Snoot snorted. "Really, *Miss Polly Loblolly?*"

Loblolly shrugged. "Point taken. It was my father Wally's idea, so my name would rhyme with his and my mother's, Holly."

"What was her maiden name? I mean, she could have kept it, right?"

Loblolly cringed. "It gets worse. Her maiden name was Holly Golleigh."

Blunt rapped his knuckles on the table. "Hey, you two, can we get back to work?"

Snoot and Loblolly began quietly sorting folders again, but after a few folders, Snoot couldn't contain herself. "Holly Golleigh Loblolly! Ha!"

Jeremy Polk stared at what appeared to be an empty autopsy table. "This just won't do."

His first thought when he returned to the morgue with the invisible body was to run her through their new forensic analyzer, the ME-4350 Array, a Rube Goldberg-like machine that could independently and sequentially conduct a full autopsy of a body, as well as gather crime scene data from the victim's clothing. The problem was the damned machine's activation sensors couldn't detect the body.

He stared at the table again, and the body continued to remain invisible. "Shit."

He walked over to a side table and retrieved a white sheet, throwing it over the body, which revealed her contours. "Well, aren't you lovely."

He grabbed a measuring tape and measured her head to toe. "Five feet seven, and if I had to guess, about one hundred twenty pounds."

He checked the weight gauge. "And I'd be off by two pounds. One hundred eighteen it is."

He pulled over a stool, sat down next to the body, and checked his watch. "Where the hell are they?"

The question was answered by the sudden opening of the double doors to the autopsy room. He was expecting Grave and Morgan, but June and Rippley were a complete surprise. "What ho, June Thursday and her amazingly invisible progeny."

June smiled at him. "We're hoping we can be of help." She looked over at the table and cringed. "Is she still invisible?"

Polk nodded. "Very much so, and I'm completely stuck. Autopsying an invisible woman is not my specialty."

Grave cleared his throat. "Rippley thinks she may be able to help."

Polk looked at her. "She's growing fast. I've never seen a three-year-old so tall. She must be over four feet."

"I am exactly four foot two, sir, but my size has little to do with my being here."

Polk raised his eyebrows. "And precociously articulate as well."

Rippley frowned. She hated the word precocious. She was what she was, intelligent and gifted. "May I see her?"

Polk pointed at the sheet-covered body, and shrugged. "Be my guest."

Rippley walked around the table, taking in the contours of the body. She closed her eyes, trying to remember the shapes of all her students. "She could be one of two students. I'm thinking Grace Gnote—we called her GiGi at the school, what with the silent G in her last name—or Ann Aesthesia, and yes, that's her real name. Both are young, in their early twenties, and about this shape and size. Grace is a ginger like me, but Ann is a platinum blonde—out of the bottle, of course." She tentatively touched the sheet. "May I take this off?"

Polk nodded. "Yes, but why?"

"I need to be able to touch her skin."

"Sure, just pull it back at the head."

"Wait," said Grave. "Is the head still, um, you know."

Polk smiled. "No, I straightened it out. She'd look normal, assuming we could see her."

Grave nodded to Rippley. "Okay, then, go on, Rip."

Rippley smirked. "That's *Rippley*, if you please. Two Ps as in *ripple*, not one P as in *Alien*. And, for the record, I detest Rip."

"Sorry," said Grave, taking a step back.

Rippley climbed up on Polk's examination stool, slowly pulled the sheet away from the woman's head, and placed a hand palm down on what should have been her forehead. "She's very cold. I wasn't expecting that."

She withdrew her hand. "Now, here's what I'm going to try. I'm going to become completely invisible, like her. Then I'll place my hand on her forehead and become visible again. With any luck, my energy will be strong enough to make her visible again. I'm not sure it will work, though. Her aura is very weak and fading fast.

"Go on then, honey," said June.

They all watched as Rippley quickly became invisible. Seconds passed and Rippley remained invisible. Then, slowly but surely, she and the dead woman began to reappear, becoming cloudlike at first and then coming into sharp focus.

Rippley looked down at her, then quickly looked away. "It's Grace," she said, then burst into tears. "My Grace."

Grave pulled the sheet down farther, revealing Grace's Skunk 'n Donuts uniform. He looked over at Morgan, who nodded silently.

10

The ride back to the Blunt's house passed in silence, save for the soft whimpering of Rippley, enveloped in June's arms. June stared blankly ahead, gently rocking her daughter.

Grave escorted them to the door. "I'll send Barry along as soon as I can."

June nodded. "Not if you need him. We have to catch this bastard." She turned and walked into the house, closing the door behind her.

Grave puffed out a big sigh and returned to the hovercruiser.

"Is she going to be all right, you think?" said Morgan.

Grave shrugged. "I don't know. She's old for her age, but then again, she's just three. I guess time will tell."

"Right, Right."

"So, cap'n, where to now? Back to the station?"

Morgan shook his head and smiled. "No, I think I'm going to do a little practice retirement and actually go home early for once." He turned and talked into the hovercruiser's control panel. "Skunk 'n Donuts, on the square." He turned back to Grave. "I couldn't help notice where you parked that damned vehicle of yours."

Grave smiled back. "I'll see if I can learn anything more about Grace from the employees there. Her schedule. Whether she seemed troubled. Etcetera."

"Sounds good. Now, as to this acting chief business."

Grave frowned at the reminder. "What?"

"Let's wait until tomorrow morning to break the news. I'll do it, first thing, so don't think to go back to the station after you leave Skunk 'n Donuts, all right?"

"Yes, sir."

Morgan turned back to the control panel. "Is this the best you can do? Faster, please, I have a date with a wood carving set."

Grave chuckled. "What, you're going to spend your retirement whittling?"

Morgan frowned. "Don't laugh. I carve a mean mallard." He turned back to the panel and hit it with his fist. "Are we going to move, or what?"

The hovercruiser lurched forward, flying through the next intersection so fast Grave had to shut his eyes. When he opened them, the outside world was a multicolored blur. "Captain, do we really have to go this fast? I'd like to make it to acting captain."

Morgan turned to the control panel again and slammed his fist on it. "Faster!"

Grave closed his eyes. There was only him, speed, and darkness, and the raucous laughter of Captain Morgan.

He wondered whether he had already fainted.

11

Wanda Perkins, a senior sales associate at Skunk 'n Donuts, saw Grave coming and did her best to pass off responsibility for new orders to her sales partner, Frank, who was bent over the donut trays filling a one-dozen box for a customer.

"Frank, get over here."

"What?" He continued filling the box. Two more Little Willy Crullers and the box would be full.

"Switch up with me for a minute."

"Why?"

Wanda started to answer, but Grave was already making eye contact with her as he pushed into the shop, a little bell announcing his entrance. He was a tall man with jet black hair and an almost goofy Dudley Do-Right demeanor. She wondered whether he wore the rumpled grey suit to lend himself an air of seriousness. Whatever the case, he was easy to spot.

She did her best to be professional to this man who always made the same request, prompting the only answer possible. "We're out of chocolate, detective, as I've told you time and time again. The chocolates go fast, usually before ten, so—"

"I'm not interested in donuts."

She blinked, not sure she was hearing him correctly. "Um, what?"

"I need to talk to someone who knows Grace Gnote."

Wanda seemed confused. "Grace?"

"Yes, do you know her?"

Wanda nodded. "Yeah, of course, she works here."

Grave looked down the row of booths along the window. There was an open one at the rear. "Can we perhaps talk back there?"

Wanda frowned. "Is something wrong?"

Grave cleared his throat and ran a finger around his collar. "Seriously, I need to talk to you back there. Now."

Wanda gave him a quick nod, and turned to Frank. "Take over for me for a few minutes."

She took off her apron and moved down the counter, Grave watching her go. He had on many occasions wondered whether he should ask her out. She was tall and beautiful, with skin so perfectly smooth and brown that Grave had often wondered whether she was a simdroid based on some famous actress, although he couldn't figure out who. In any case, he never got up the courage to approach her in any way other than a fervent demand for chocolate donuts.

Wanda slipped into the booth, and Grave sat down opposite her. "I'm afraid I have some bad news."

Wanda shook her head, anger spreading over her face. "He hurt her again, didn't he?"

Grave blinked. "He?"

"Her ex. She took a restraining order out on him, but he still hangs around."

"Do you have a name for him?"

"Yeah, Cliff Gnote."

Grave took out a notepad and pencil. "Address?"

"No, they split a year ago. I don't know where that shithead lives. So, how bad is it?"

"I'm afraid she's dead, Wanda. Killed over there on the square last night."

Wanda sat back in the booth, mouth open, tears forming. She looked out the window. Crime scene tape fluttered in the breeze around a large section of the square. "I was wondering about that. Shit, she didn't deserve that."

"When was the last time you saw her?"

Wanda sighed and brushed away a tear, her voice shaky. "Um, last night. She finished up her shift at eight."

"Did she seem concerned about anything? Was she acting unusual?"

"No, in fact, she was looking forward to meeting with her friend Ann. They sat right here in this booth." She cringed. "Makes me not want to sit here."

"We're almost done. Do you have a last name for this Ann?"

Wanda raised an eyebrow. "Don't laugh, her name's Ann Aesthesia."

Grave laughed despite himself. "Why do parents do that to their kids?"

"Yeah, right," said Wanda, growing serious. "Anyway, I don't know how long they talked, because I was on my way out. End of my shift, too. But what I can tell you is that when I went outside and walked past the window, I could see they were arguing about something."

Grave cocked his head. "Any idea what?"

"No, not a clue. I mean, it wasn't a yelling and screaming kind of argument. It was just, um, heated, you know. They were leaning in, going at each other."

"Do you know where I can find Ann?"

She shook her head. "Not a clue. No, wait, they both went to some ridiculous school where you learn to be—get this—*invisible*. I mean, what a crock."

Grave nodded. "I know the school."

"Seriously, is it on the up and up? I'd certainly like to disappear around here some days."

"Yes, maybe you should give it a try. Then you can disappear every time you see me."

She blushed. "Nothing personal."

"I know, it's all about the chocolate donuts."

"I keep tellin' you—"

"I know, 'get in before ten.'"

She smiled. "Exactly."

Grave rapped his knuckles on the table. "Okay, let's get back to Ann. What does she look like?"

"Oh, she's a real looker. Tall, shapely, with a gorgeous face and can't-miss-it platinum blond hair."

Grave closed his notebook. "Okay, I think we're done here, Wanda."

She smiled at him and slipped out of the booth. "Meet me at the register."

Grave blinked. "What? Why?"

She gave him a little wink. "Just meet me, okay?"

Grave nodded and slipped out of the booth as she went behind the counter and into the back room, where Grave surmised the baking was done.

She appeared moments later with a little bag. "I was saving it for my Dad, but here, the very last chocolate donut of the day."

Grave took the bag eagerly. "Thank you so much."

"Just do one thing for me," she said, putting her hands on her hips. "Yes?"

"You find that bastard and lock his ass up!"

"We'll do our best."

Wanda shook her head vigorously. "No, you promise me you're going to nail his ass."

Grave nodded. "If he's the killer, I promise you."

"Good, good," she said, "And I'll promise you there will always be a chocolate donut for you here, day or night."

"Thank you." He raised the little bag, gave her a friendly smile, and walked into the night. Maybe he *would* ask her out.

12

Officer Larry, Badge 67, felt something odd in his circuits and wondered whether he had made a mistake going with a black market upgrade from the Krypto Knights, a hovercycle gang noted for all things cyber. They called it an ambition upgrade and said he might feel a tingle from time to time as the upgrade rolled out in his various systems, particularly as emotions were adjusted up from low simdroid levels to near-human levels.

He felt like he should cry, but he had no capacity to do so. He felt like he should shout in anger, and did, startling a nearby squirrel gathering his last nut of the day. A giggle suddenly escaped his synthetic lips, forcing him to clasp a hand over his mouth. *A mood swing,* he thought, *how strange.*

Most important, he had a feeling of importance and pride—he could do this. He could impress the powers that be that among all the simdroid officers, he should be considered for a new role as detective. They already had two simdroid detectives, Charlize Holmes and Smithers-Watson. Charlize had started her career as a personal assistant and sometime auto mechanic to Detective Simon Grave, and Smithers-Watson had been nothing more than a butler at the Hawthorne Mansion. So why not a third simdroid detective, and why not him?

LenBoswell

He shouted in anger again, and it felt good. It felt right. He could do this. He *would* do this. And they'd have no choice but to recognize his skills and promote him to detective.

"What are you doing out here," said Grave, startling him.

Larry tried to stay simdroid calm, but the new programming had him shaking with nerves. "Um, well, you startled me, sir."

Grave cocked his head. "You were shouting."

"Yes, sir."

"And it sounded angry."

Larry saw his chance. "Yes, sir. Who wouldn't be angry about the murder of that poor woman?"

Grave nodded. "Indeed. But what are you doing out on the square at this hour? All the other Larrys have retired for the night."

Larry attempted a sigh and found that it relieved the pressure he was feeling, at least somewhat. "I want to help, sir. Her personal drone is missing, as are her personal effects: purse, etcetera. I thought I would look around, ask around, see if we've missed anything in our initial sweep of the area."

Grave squinted at him. "I've never met a simdroid officer—any Larry—who displayed such initiative."

Larry looked down at the ground. "Sorry, sir."

"No, no," said Grave. "I like it." He looked around the square. He and Larry were the only police in the area. "Continue with your search, Officer Larry."

Larry smiled, and it felt like more than a tug of wires and springs. *Is this what they call happiness?* "Yes, sir."

"Good night, then, Larry." Grave turned to go, but then turned back. "I'd like you at the morning briefing tomorrow."

"Sir?"

"To report on what you find or don't find tonight."

"Yes, sir, I'll be there."

Grave turned and walked away, making his way across the square to his little sports car.

Officer Larry watched him slip into the car and start it up, the sound of gospel music blaring across the square. He felt a tingle, something new, some as yet experienced emotion. He felt *annoyed.*

37

13

Sergeant Blunt's personal drone, Object, ended the call with Captain Morgan and returned to his place in the corner to discuss the situation with the other drones, Midnight and Pine Cone.

Blunt returned to the table where he, Loblolly, and Snoot had been sorting student folders. They had separated the files into men, boys, women, and girls, and then sorted them alphabetically. "That was Captain Morgan. We have the victim's name, Grace Gnote."

"Awesome," said Loblolly. "Woman or girl?"

"Woman," said Blunt.

Snoot grabbed the women's stack and thumbed through it. "Nothing here."

"Oh," said Blunt. "The G is silent in Gnote."

Snoot smirked. "Grace Guh-Note, it is." She looked higher in the stack and pulled out the right folder. "Here we go."

She opened the folder. There was a copy of Grace's application stapled on the left side of the folder and a photograph of her on the right. "Wow, a real looker. Man, I'd kill to have that red hair of hers."

"Let me see," said Loblolly.

Snoot held up the folder so Loblolly and Blunt could see.

"A damned shame," said Loblolly.

Blunt frowned and shook his head. "I remember her. She seemed beaten down on her first day, but by the time she graduated, she was a different person—confident and happy."

"Right," said Snoot, "and now we have our prime suspect."

"Wait, what?" said Loblolly.

"Right here in the application under reason for applying, and I quote: *to avoid my ex.*"

"Does it say who that is?" said Loblolly.

Snoot scanned the application, looking for more information. "Nope."

"I remember talking with June about her. She was having trouble with her ex-husband, who had abused her. She had taken out a restraining order against him, but he had continued to harass her."

"Bastard," said Loblolly.

"But he shouldn't be too hard to find," said Snoot. "We should be able to lay our hands on that order pretty quickly."

"Let's do it," said Loblolly, pushing back from the table.

Blunt held up a hand. "Whoa, whoa, whoa. The captain said we are to do nothing more today. He wants an all-hands meeting first thing tomorrow morning to discuss assignments and next steps."

"Well shit, Barry. The guy could be hundreds of miles away by then," said Snoot.

Blunt shook his head. "He was quite insistent that we stand down until morning."

Snoot huffed. "But can't we at least find the order, so we know the guy's name and address? You know we're going to have to bring him in, right?"

"I know, I know," said Blunt. "Okay, see what you can find out."

Snoot and Loblolly scrambled to their feet and raced to the door, Midnight and Pine Cone in pursuit.

Blunt called after them. "But don't you *dare* go after him."

They made no reply, but he could hear them running through the office. He shouted again. "The captain *has his reasons.*"

He could hear the door to the station open and slam shut. They were gone, heading for the courthouse.

Blunt picked up the folder, looked at the photo of Grace again, and tossed the folder back onto the table. "I sure *hope* he has his reasons."

14

Grave had to be careful not to make the turn into his old neighborhood, where he was permanently persona non grata to the homeowner's association, which had an understandable but unfortunate opinion of gospel music played at volume eleven.

It was just as well. Grave had grown tired of the house, an old bungalow with perpetual plumbing problems and a backyard giving way to the encroachment of the Chesapeake Bay, which was drowning the land at a rate of five feet a year. Grave figured he only had about ten years left before water started flooding his basement. In an unusual display of common sense, he had complied with the homeowner's association's demand that he move the hell out of the neighborhood.

And he had displayed even commoner good sense by snapping up the Crab Cove Lighthouse, which had been taken out of service thanks to the lights atop an array of thirty taller wind turbines a mile offshore. And the commonest good sense of all was that the lighthouse was situated on a remote spit of land, atop a hill fifty feet above the waterline. He would not only be safe from the sea, but would also be safe from homeowner's associations or homeowners in general, the closest home more than two miles away.

The voice of the Reverend Bendigo Bottoms suddenly boomed on the radio, offering up one of his mini-sermons between gospel selections. The reverend was dead now, firmly ensconced in the Crab

Cove Cinema Cemetery, his sermons on perpetual rerun, but Grave had had more than a few conversations with his ghost—about the meaning of life, of death, and of love. Grave visited him often at the cemetery, as well as his best ghost friend, Victoria, daughter of the founder of the town, and dead since the eighteenth century. She was a charming little girl, permanently fixed at ten years old. Maybe eleven, tops.

The reverend's mini-sermon tonight was about the importance of loving thy neighbor as you would love yourself. Grave couldn't help noting that there was nary a mention of homeowner's associations.

He made the turn onto Lighthouse Lane and drove on, steadily climbing up the hill to his new home, which was currently part of another spectacular sunset. The sound of the gospel music actually seemed to diminish as it began to compete with the steady thrum of the windmills offshore.

Grave pulled the Sprite into the small six-car parking lot and guided it to a stop in the light-keeper's reserved space, another perk of the purchase, not that he was expecting competition or the return of the now-retired light-keeper.

He put his hand into the fingerprint reader and the front door clicked open, the smell of salt and aging paint greeting him. He pushed the door open wide to let Barry fly in, then stepped in and closed the door. He could hear his dog, Lucky the Wonder Dog, a crab hound who resembled the Luck Dragon, clattering down the spiral staircase that looped around the walls of the lighthouse.

"Here, boy," he said, but Lucky didn't need any help finding him. The dog bounded down the final steps and leaped into Grave's arms, licking him with his rough tongue.

Grave laughed. "Good boy, good boy."

He put him down and gave him a scratch behind the ears. "What have you been up to today? And where's Roderick?"

"Over here," said Roderick, his head suddenly appearing from behind a stack of as-yet-unpacked boxes. He was a simdroid, manservant class, with special skills in cooking, dog walking, and housekeeping. Grave could have chosen from among several models, but the model that resembled an old actor, Peter Lorre, seemed perfect for a lighthouse environment. Like the actor, he was short, slightly hunched, and had eyes that seemed to be bugging out of his head. There was almost a Hunchback of Notre Dame creepiness about him. He smiled at the wrong times, and his whispery voice formed and stretched words beyond breaking, emphasis often placed on the wrong syllable. *Did you get the in-for-MA-tion?*

"Ah, there you are," said Grave. "How did Lucky behave today?"

Roderick smiled ruefully, a slight twitch forming at the corner of his mouth. "He made a mistake or two. Left a few *gifts* for me, but nothing unusual for a dog trying to acclimate to a new space. And how was your day?"

The fact that he was now acting chief suddenly slammed into him like a ton of rocks. "Fine."

"I heard you coming, so I've uncorked a fresh bottle of Duct Tape Chardonnay for you. Dinner should be ready in about twenty minutes."

"Good, good," said Grave, walking to the stairs.

"Oh, and I've managed to fix the stair lift. You can ride up now if you wish."

Grave considered the options, weighing his desire to get more fit by stair-climbing against his desire to just slump into his favorite chair.

The stair lift was the easy choice. He strapped himself in and pushed the start button, the chair suddenly lurching upwards at great speed. "Yikes."

Roderick called after him. "Push the lever back for slow."

Grave grabbed the lever and pulled it back, slowing the chair in its spiral ascent. He leaned back, trying to relax, as the chair went from level to level. Level one was a small living room with a couch, a recliner, and a Surround System that was currently playing *Casablanca*. Peter Lorre was talking to Humphrey Bogart about something. Grave had never watched the picture all the way through. He had just seen snippets of it, as he did now. Roderick, however, seemed to be endlessly fascinated by his doppelganger.

"Here's to you, kid," said Grave as the stair lift rose to the next level, a small kitchen and dining room. The table was set for dinner, including the bottle of Duct Tape Chardonnay—Slogan: *The wine that can fix anything.*

Grave stopped the lift, walked over to the table, and poured himself a large glass of wine. He took a quick sip. "Ah, just right," he said, returning to the lift and accelerating to the third level, his bedroom, where Roderick had laid out a pair of jeans and a polo shirt.

Grave stopped the lift and got out. Rather than changing clothes, he decided to just take off his gray suit jacket, and climb the short flight of stairs to the observation deck. The hatch to the deck opened easily, and he managed to climb out without spilling much of his wine.

The sunset was spectacular, the sky orange, amber, yellow, and violet, in a progression he could not follow but only wonder at, the ability of light and clouds to conspire in a display that was never repeated twice but always entertained. Even the wind turbines seemed to be part of the show, golden beams glinting off their blades as they continued to thrum along without surcease.

A voice behind him made him startle and spill what would have been a significant gulp of his wine.

"Greetings, Grave. How's it hanging?"

Grave knew the voice well, so he was not surprised to see a large sentient seagull perched on the railing. "Not so well, Horace. How about you?"

Horace spread his wings, then ruffled his feathers. "Never better, sir, never better, although I could use a french-fry or six."

Grave chuckled. "I bet you could, but what brings you here? I thought you were working on some hush-hush project with the military."

Horace reverted to bird behavior, letting loose an angry scream. "They wanted to frickin' *weaponize* me, and I'm just not down with that."

Grave nodded. "Not surprised—with either." He had come to know Horace well after apprehending him for leading a flock of seagulls against drones hovering near Le Crabe Bleu, the town's only French restaurant. Horace had subsequently helped him solve the murder of Chase "Superman" Arnold, president of the Krypto Knights hovercycle gang. Horace's intelligence and speaking ability were all thanks to the late Lachlan McLachlan, inventor of the neural node, which amplified intelligence and provided communications technology designed to replace personal drones. Neural nodes had become the new new thing, even in Crab Cove, where most citizens tried to hold the future at bay for as long as possible. The early adopters were easy to spot; for one thing, they didn't have personal drones hovering near them; and for another, they startled when a call came through, their bodies shaking as if in a fit; and finally and most noticeably, they moved their lips as their node and their brains conspired to answer the call without audible speech. It was freaky.

"Are you okay?" said Horace.

Grave startled. "What?"

"You seemed to be zoned out there."

"Oh, just thinking. So why aren't you down by the boardwalk, searching for fries?"

Horace bobbed his head. "I should be, shouldn't I? But there's the matter of the military. They didn't exactly let me go."

"So you're on the run?"

"More like on the wing, but the result is the same. I'm a fugitive, it seems."

Grave nodded, knowing what would come next. "So you're looking for a place to crash for a few days?"

"Ah, Grave, you are a master of deduction. May I?"

Grave considered the downside, because he couldn't see much of an upside. "Well, there's the matter of my drone, Barry."

Horace squawked. "Oh, him. No, we'll be fine. I've come to terms with drones and a crowded sky."

"And my dog."

Horace cocked his head. "You have a dog? What kind of dog?"

"His name is Lucky, and he's a crab hound."

Horace flapped his wings. "I hate those little slithery dogs. They steal crabs from us."

"Then maybe you should find another place to hide out."

Horace shook his head. "Oh, no, no, please, I'll give him wide berth. No problem. Seriously, no problem."

Grave sighed. "Well, there's more, I'm afraid."

Horace cocked his head. "Oh? Go on, what?"

"I have a new manservant, a simdroid named Roderick. He's intentionally a neat freak, so you'll have to pick up any stray feathers and do your business outside."

"No worries there, sir. The military folks had similar concerns, so—tadah!—I'm toilet trained."

Grave raised an eyebrow. "Toilet trained?"

"Yes, so long as you remember to put the seat down, I'll be fine."

Grave tried not to think about it. "Okay, but there's one more thing."

"Jeez, Grave, how many *things* do you have?"

"Just one more where you're concerned. The lighthouse came with a stipulation."

"What kind of stipulation?"

"I took ownership in the middle of a federal research project on crab populations in the Crab Cove Conservation Zone."

Horace cocked his head. "So?"

"So the project was—or rather still is—based in this lighthouse."

"I don't get it. What does this have to do with me?"

"Nothing, really. It's just that the chief researcher is a simcrab, a crab-sized carcinologist droid named Red."

"So you don't want me to happen upon him and peck him to pieces."

Grave nodded. "Yes, exactly. But don't worry, he mostly keeps to himself on the first level. That is, when he's not in the water."

"Okay, you have my word. No pecking Red."

Grave looked at his watch. "All right, then, you can stay."

Horace leaped into the air, flew in a circle around the top of the lighthouse, and landed again on the railing. "Yippee!"

"Hold your yippee for now. We still have to break the news to Barry, Lucky, and Roderick."

"Of course, of course, and I assure you, I will be on my best behavior."

"All right, let's go down. Dinner should be ready now."

"Mm, will there be french-fries?"

Grave laughed. "There can be, I guess. The synthesizer should be able to handle that."

"Synthesizer? Ugh, I hate syn-fries. They taste like *vegetables*."

"Well, you know what they say about beggars and their ability to choose."

Horace sighed. "Okay, point taken. Now, back to you. What's so bad about today? Why so glum?"

Grave sighed and gulped down the rest of the Duct Tape Chardonnay. He wondered whether it could actually fix this, somehow make him *not* the acting chief. "It's a long story."

"I'm all ears. No, wait, I'm not."

Grave managed a laugh. "No, that's true. Anyway, let's go down to dinner. All shall be revealed."

"Like the chocolate on your face?"

15

Officer Larry stood on the gazebo and surveyed the scene. It was just past eleven, and the last of the band members had just loaded his drums into a van and driven away. The crowd that had gathered to watch and listen to the Crab Cove Saturday Night Concert was long gone but had left the square littered with all manner of trash. And try as he might to prevent them, the crowd had quickly swelled, ignoring the crime scene tape and forever spoiling the scene. He just hoped the forensic team had all the clues it needed.

He leaned down and picked up a concert poster that someone had thrown away. Tonight's concert had featured four bands, the Crabaires, Carl and the Crabtones, Metal Mallet, and the featured performer, Sim City Slim, a simdroid performer who specialized in country-rap fusion. He crumpled the poster and tossed it in a nearby trashcan. Time to get back to business.

The victim's purse and drone were still missing. A purse could be anywhere, spirited away by anyone who happened upon it, even if they had nothing to do with the murder. There was a homeless shelter opposite the east side of the square, across Imperial Avenue, right next to the community parking lot. Someone in the shelter might have it, or someone—anyone—could have found it, got into their car, and disappeared.

47

The drone was another matter. It was programmed to stay within a few feet of its owner, unless directed otherwise, and even then, there were limits to its effective range. Given the square's dimensions, being just one block square, it was doubtful that a working drone would be anywhere but in the square.

On the other hand, there was every reason for the murderer to take both the purse and the drone. Taking the purse would slow down identification of the body, and taking the drone would assure that no one got its sound and voice recorder or its video records. On yet another hand, however, the crime was quick and brutal, so maybe the murderer left the scene without taking the purse or the drone. The black market for drones was alive and well in Crab Cove, so that was also a possibility.

Officer Larry sighed in a way that almost approximated a human sigh, but rather than trailing off at the end, as it well should, the sigh ended abruptly in an unsigh-like way, as if a switch had been thrown. He ignored his failed sigh and considered what to do next. He wanted to bring something to tomorrow morning's all-staff meeting, but he had nothing. He had covered the entire square with his scanners, but there was no sign of the purse or the drone—just a wealth of trash. The logical thing to do next would be to view the CCTV footage, but as he understood it, Charlize and Smithers-Watson were already doing that.

He had interviewed the two chess players earlier, and they had seen nothing. He had searched all the trashcans, dumpsters, and alleys around the square and come up empty. Then he had an idea, an idea so bright and shiny that he could feel his hydraulic fluid course a little faster. The murder had been swift, meaning the killer, whether he was invisible or not, would have positioned himself as close to the victim's path as possible.

He trotted down the steps of the gazebo and walked over to the spot where they'd found the body. Then he slowly turned in a circle, trying to find the closest place to hide. The closest object was one of the benches that circled the gazebo, but it wouldn't be a good place to hide. Just beyond that was the chess table, but that would have been occupied by the two chess players. The only other hiding spot was the gazebo itself. Not on the gazebo, of course, but just out of sight on ground level. The murderer could have peeked around the corner of the gazebo and quickly covered the ground to the victim. And the angle was such that the two chess players wouldn't have seen anything.

Officer Larry smiled. Now he had something to share. He scanned the square one last time—nothing and no one—and began walking to the community parking lot and his police hovercruiser. Just as he passed the gazebo, he tripped and fell to the ground. He scrambled to his feet and looked down at the ground behind him. Nothing. Then he dropped to his knees and began probing the grass with his hands. Inches away and a few inches off the ground, his hand touched something soft and wet.

And invisible.

16

Grave and Morgan stood beside Polk and Officer Larry and watched as the forensics team loaded the blanket-draped body into the ambulance.

"I best be going," said Polk.

"Any thoughts?" said Morgan.

Polk shook his head. "Not much, seeing that she's invisible. Feeling around the body I can definitely say we're looking at but not seeing a young woman who's been stabbed to death. Thing is, though, there's hardly any blood, so I'd have to say she was moved here."

"Killed somewhere else, then?" said Grave.

"Yes, that's my take on it. Anyway, I hate to say this, but I'm going to need Rippley again tomorrow morning. See if she can make this poor woman's body visible."

Morgan sighed. "Yes, damned shame. She's already traumatized, but. . ."

"No," said Grave, "she's tougher than she looks, at least when you can see her. I'll give Blunt a call and have him bring her and June in for tomorrow morning's meeting. Polk, if you're available, we can go over the first killing and then go back to the morgue for a look-see."

"That works for me," said Polk. "All right, till tomorrow." He turned away and headed for the ambulance.

Grave turned to Morgan and Officer Larry. "I have a theory about who the second victim is."

"Oh?" said Morgan.

"Yes, on Friday night she was seen having an argument with a woman in Skunk 'n Donuts, just half an hour or so before she was murdered."

"And you know who that is?"

"Yes, another of Rippley's students, Ann Aesthesia."

"Holy Christ," said Morgan.

"Indeed," said Grave. He turned to Officer Larry. "Good work tonight."

"Thank you, sir."

Morgan scoffed. "Except for one thing. What the hell happened here? It looks like a garbage truck exploded on our crime scene."

Larry looked down. "Sorry, sir. It was the concert. There was just no crowd control, and there was just me, and—"

Grave patted him on the shoulder. "No worries, Larry, we've all been there. Now, you were here all night. Were you able to find the purse or the drone, or anything, for that matter?"

Larry shook his head. "No, sir. I looked everywhere. All over the square and up and down the nearby streets and alleys. Even scanned the entire square."

"Wait," said Morgan. "How could you do all that with such a big crowd of people?"

"Oh, no," said Larry. "I completed the scans just before people started showing up. Covered every inch of this square."

"What time was it?" said Grave. "When you completed the scan."

"Ah," said Larry, "I see where you're going. I completed the scan at about six forty-five, so that means whoever killed this new victim placed the body here after that time."

"I don't get it," said Morgan. "If the crowd was so big, surely someone would have tripped over the body."

"Well, then," said Larry. "The concert broke up at around ten, and the square was clear of everyone but me by eleven."

"So," said Grave, "we'll have to check the CCTV footage for that one-hour period. Larry, Charlize and Smithers-Watson are already working on the footage from Friday night. Can you gather up the new footage first thing tomorrow morning and bring it to the meeting?"

Larry beamed. "Of course, sir. You can count on me—always."

"Good," said Grave. "Off you go, then. You've put in quite a productive day."

"Yes, sir, thank you, sir." He turned and started walking toward the parking lot.

Grave turned to Morgan. "I like him. He might be useful in the coming days."

Morgan raised his eyebrows. "How so? He's just another Officer Larry. We have scores of him."

"No, seriously, there's something different about him. I'm thinking maybe we can use him as a detective."

Morgan looked astounded. "A *detective*? A *Larry* as a detective?"

"Yes, a junior detective, mind, but I think he has potential."

Morgan shook his head. "Well, you're the acting chief, so whatever floats your boat."

Grave chuckled. "Okay, then, you have to tell me about that massive bandage on your finger. Looks like a white lollipop."

Morgan held it up and rolled his eyes. "This retirement thing is not going well, particularly as it relates to whittling."

"Well, at least you've got the cargo shorts and Hawaiian shirt working for you. Nice parrots, by the way."

17

Captain Henry Morgan could have worn his shorts and Hawaiian shirt to the all-staff meeting on Sunday morning, but he decided it would look better if he showed up in his standard, workaday uniform. He cleared his throat, trying to get the attention of his team. "Good morning."

A mumble of muted *good mornings* came back at him.

"I know it's unusual to have you all here on a Sunday morning, but three events bring us here this morning. First and foremost, we have *two* murders on our hands now.

A murmur of surprised *twos* came back at him.

"We'll get to those in some detail, but first I have a somewhat major announcement, at least for me. As of the end of the month, I will retire from my position as Chief of Police.

A chorus of gasps came back at him. *What? Oh, no!*

"Now, now, everyone's time comes sooner or later. I've a nice little houseboat picked out, and I plan to spend my days fishing off the back of it."

Stunned silence had set in, most people shaking their heads and staring at the floor.

"Until then, I'll be on terminal leave. Which leads me to the next announcement. The city council has formed a team to find and recruit my replacement. In the interim, Detective Simon Grave will be acting chief. So, until a replacement is named, Grave is your go-to guy."

Stunned silence continued, even though the subject had changed. *Disbelief* seemed to be the dominant expression on the faces of the detectives and officers. *Grave? Why him? What the—*

"And with that, I'll turn this meeting, and this station, over into the capable hands of Detective Grave." He motioned Grave forward. "Simon, it's all yours."

Silence continued to reign supreme. Mouths were now open as the reality of the situation set in and Grave stepped forward.

Grave looked out at them and had the overwhelming feeling that he now knew what it would be like to face a firing squad. "Thank you, Captain Morgan, and I'm sure I speak for everyone in regretting your departure while wishing you the very best retirement."

Morgan gave everyone a quick nod, then turned back to Grave, urging him to continue.

"There will be time for speeches at his retirement party. Details on that to follow. Now, one other announcement before we get to the murders."

He looked over at Detective Snoot, who suddenly looked worried. *What's he up to?*

"The council values our input and wants us at the table during the hiring process. With that in mind, we have selected Detective Amanda Snoot to represent us in the review of internal and external candidates."

Snoot flushed with disappointment and then anger. *Why me? What the—*

Grave tried not to look at her; he knew she'd be on top of him the moment the meeting ended. "And speaking of internal candidates, let me put your minds at ease, I will not be a candidate. My role is to fill the gap, then get back to my role as detective. I seek nothing more."

Relief seemed to be the operative word now, as a chorus of relieved sighs spread throughout the room, as if they'd all miraculously dodged a bullet.

"Because of my new role, there will be some minor adjustments to working teams, but I'll get to that in a moment. For now, anyone not directly working on the recent homicides should get back to their jobs.

Homicide teams, Polk, June, and Rippley, let's take a fifteen minute break, then reform here." He turned to Snoot. "Snoot, captain's office, please."

Mumbling and whispers of *what's next* followed the crowd from the room. Grave watched them go, then realized he needed to see one other officer. "Wait, I need to see Officer Larry as well."

Twenty Officer Larrys stopped in their tracks, not sure if Grave was talking about them.

Grave realized his mistake. "I mean, the Officer Larry I spoke with last night at the crime scene."

Nineteen Officer Larrys resumed their movement toward the door as one Officer Larry stood there in the middle of the room, a finger pointing at his chest and a smile growing on his face. "Me?"

18

Snoot stormed out of the captain's office, leaving Grave standing there, his arms raised in an appeal for her to come back. But she didn't. He had tried to explain why she was selected—her toughness, her intelligence, her knowledge of the team, and the skills and temperament needed by a new chief—but she just sat there seething and scoffing at every point Grave tried to make.

Detective Loblolly peeked in the office. "Okay to come in?"

Grave nodded and slumped back in his chair. "Yes, of course."

They could both hear the door to the station slam shut, hard.

"Well, that went well," said Loblolly.

Grave snorted. "Yeah, right."

She sat down opposite him. "Look, I think you made a good decision. She really is the best one to represent us. Not going to take any crap off anyone on the selection team."

"I know, but I wish she could see that."

She stood back up and looked at her watch. "Conference room in five?"

Grave nodded.

"Okay, and don't worry. I'll talk to her tonight, have drinks. It will be fine."

Grave smiled at her and tried to imagine sitting across a table from her, sharing a bottle of Duct Tape Chardonnay. That really might fix everything. "Thanks, Polly."

She nodded and left the office.

Grave looked down at the papers on Captain Morgan's desk. That was going to be the worst part. All the damned paperwork.

"Excuse me," said Officer Larry, rapping his knuckles on the doorframe. "You wanted to see me?"

Grave looked up and smiled. "Yes, come on in and have a seat."

Larry moved to the chair and sat down.

"A couple of things, Larry. First, were you able to get the CCTV tapes for Saturday night?"

"Yes, sir, just gave them to Detective Holmes."

"Okay, great. Now, how long have you been with the force?"

Larry blinked. "Three years, seven months, four days, two hours, forty-one minutes, and thirty-four seconds."

Grave held up his hands, hoping Larry wouldn't start ticking off the seconds. "Great, great. Now, the work you've done over the past two days has been exceptional in my view."

"Thank you, sir. Just trying to do my part. Solve crimes and such."

"Indeed." He looked Larry up and down. The man really was the spitting image of Morgan Freeman, as were the other Larrys. "So, are you ready to take the next step?"

"Sir?"

"To detective. Would you like to be a detective?"

Larry beamed. "Yes, sir!"

"On a trial basis, mind. Do a good job, and we'll make it permanent."

Larry nodded, his enthusiasm undiminished. "Yes, of course."

"All right, then." He opened the top drawer on the desk, pulled out a gold Crab Cove detective shield, and slid it in Larry's direction.

Larry scooped it up before it could fly off the desk.

"Couple of things now, Larry."

"Yes, sir."

"After today, no more officer uniform. A sport coat and slacks will be fine, but really, anything that makes you feel comfortable in your new role."

Larry looked concerned. "Um, I don't have any other clothes. No Larry does. The uniform is part of what makes us all Larrys."

"Which brings me to the second change you'll need to make."

"Second change?"

"Yes, your name. Larry will no longer do. You need a new name."

Larry sat back in his chair. "Wow, I never thought I'd have to change my name."

"But you can see why, right? I can't be calling out for Larry, expecting you to come, and have nineteen other Larrys scrambling into my office."

Larry nodded. "I see what you mean, sir. Yes, a new name."

"Any ideas?"

Larry shook his head. "No, sir, but can I think about it?"

"Sure, just have different clothes and a different name when you check in tomorrow morning."

"Okay, I can do that."

"Great," said Grave, glancing at his watch. "Oops, we're a little late. Time to head back to the conference room."

They both stood and walked to the door.

"Sir," said Larry. "One thing. Can I have a last name, too?"

Grave shrugged. "Sure, and a middle name if you like."

Larry smiled. "Thank you, sir. And I won't let you down, sir."

Grave hoped he wouldn't. "You'll be fine. Now, let's get to it. We have a couple of murder cases to solve."

19

Officer Larry seemed delighted, but Detective Polly Loblolly seemed crushed and crestfallen when Grave announced the new pairings and assignments under his acting captaincy.

With Snoot off to the City Council deliberations, Grave assigned Officer Larry to team up with Loblolly. They would have principal investigatory responsibility for the murder of Grace Gnote. Detectives Charlize Holmes and Smithers-Watson would continue as a team, with responsibility for the second murder as well as everything related to the Surround Vision versions of the CCTV tapes for both murders.

Grave and Sergeant Blunt, meanwhile, would stay at the station to coordinate the investigations and provide assistance as needed. For his part, Blunt would have to stay out of the investigations because of his conflict of interest with Rippley's school. Rippley and her mother, June, would provide technical assistance on all things invisibility but would not participate in the actual grunt work of the investigations.

With that all decided, Grave turned to Jeremy Polk, ME, for his forensics report. "Jeremy, what can you tell us so far?"

Polk took a deep breath, which seemed to puff him up, making him look slightly taller than the diminutive man he was. "We have two murders, clearly connected, at least by invisibility, and both challenging from a forensics standpoint. First, let's discuss Victim One, Ms. Gnote.

The first challenge was returning her to visibility, and I'd like to thank Rippley Blunt for doing just that."

He paused and gave a nod to Rippley, who nodded back and smiled.

"Now," said Polk, "with her returned to visibility, we were able to process her body through the ME-4350 Forensic Analyzer Array, or the FAA for short."

He paused again, looking around the conference table to see if they had been impressed. They just stared back at him blankly.

"So, cause of death was definitely a broken neck. FAA estimated the force required to inflict the resultant damage and determined that the *least* possible amount of force had been applied. To do that, the murderer, whether man *or woman*, would have had to have military or martial arts training. The particular hold employed involved grabbing the victim's jaw with one hand and her forehead with the other, and then giving her head a quick snap to the left. I have an animation if you'd like to see it."

"Not right now, Polk," said Grave. "Please continue. Any DNA evidence?"

Polk smirked. He didn't like to be told what he should cover next, even though Grave had guessed exactly what he was going to talk about next: DNA. "Yes, yes, the DNA. As far as that goes, we did find hairs on her clothing, and those turned out to be a woman's hair and a man's hair. FAA was unable to match the DNA to any DNA in its database, so I'm afraid you'll have to do the legwork in identifying likely suspects."

"Anything else?"

"Just what you'd expect from someone who worked in a donut shop: a few sprinkles, powdered sugar, cinnamon, jelly, various food colorings, and chocolate."

The image of a chocolate donut appeared in Grave's brain, causing an almost instant drool response. He wiped his mouth and nodded at Polk. "Okay, what about Victim Two?"

Polk shook his head. "Still invisible, I'm afraid. We'll need Rippley's help again in that regard." He turned to Rippley. "If you're up for it, my dear."

"I am," said Rippley. "Can we go to the morgue now?"

"In a minute," said Grave. "And thank you again for helping us with this. I know it's distressing for you." He turned back to Polk. "Can you tell us *anything?*"

Polk sighed. "Just what you already know. The victim was killed elsewhere, then disposed of or staged on the square. Just from physical manipulation of the body, I can report multiple stab wounds consistent with a large knife."

Detective Charlize Holmes suddenly startled. "Large? Do you think it could have been a Bowie knife?"

Polk smiled at her. "I thought you'd make that connection, detective. Yes, it could be the work of our nemesis, serial killer Chester Clink."

Grave thought just that. The elusive Chester Clink had murdered more than 150 women up and down the Atlantic seaboard, including several in Crab Cove and the Greater Crabopolis. The last they had encountered him was over a year ago, when he escaped Charlize's grasp with the help of a getaway submarine.

Grave cleared his throat. "Which is why I assigned you and Smithers to the second murder. You're working the Clink case and will be in the best position to tell us one way or the other whether he was involved."

Polk bristled. "Well, I think the FAA will have something to say about that as well. Pretty easy to identify a Clink victim."

"Yes, of course," said Grave. "We all appreciate you and the FAA. Now, anything else?"

"No," said Polk.

"I have something," said Smithers-Watson. "Yes, it's possible we're dealing with Clink, but the first murder is completely unlike him and the second is mere speculation at this point. We have to be open to the possibility of two murderers and neither of them Chester Clink."

Grave nodded. "Good points, and I guess time will tell. Now, a question for you, Charlize. Where are you on the CCTV tapes?"

"Getting there. We tried testing the Surround Vision in this conference room earlier today, and the images were just too small to see much of anything. We need a bigger facility."

June raised her hand. "I can help with that. Ramrod Stadium is equipped with Surround Vision for major off-season events and concerts, and the playing field and sidelines are large enough to accommodate the dimensions of town square."

Charlize cocked her head. "You can do that?"

"Yes, I work at Ramrod Robotics, remember, and it's a part owner in the Crab Cove Red Claws. I'll just talk to the boss. When would you like to set it up?"

"As soon as possible," said Grave.

"But at night," said Charlize, "to get the best simulation."

June nodded. "Can't be tonight, but Monday night shouldn't be a problem. Will that work?"

"Absolutely," said Grave, "and thank you, June."

He turned back to the group. "Okay, let's split up. Charlize and Smithers, please accompany Rippley and June to the morgue." He turned to Loblolly. "Loblolly, that leaves you and Larry to start working the Gnote case."

Loblolly waived a piece of paper in front of her. "Snoot and I managed to get a copy of the restraining order on Cliff Gnote. We have his address, so I think that's the best place to start. Bring him in for questioning."

Grave shook his head. "Question him, but don't bring him in yet. I think we should all see the CCTV Surround Vision before we get too serious about suspects."

"But he's a wife beater, and he's violated the restraining order."

"Even so, don't bring him in. See what he has to say, his alibi, how he behaves under questioning, and we'll go from there after we see the tapes."

He looked from team to team. "Okay, that leaves me and Blunt here at the station. If you need anything or have something to report, we're here for you."

He looked around the room. "Okay, then, let's get out there and solve some murders."

20

Grave felt like he was on an island surrounded by open seas from horizon to horizon, but he was actually sitting at Captain Morgan's desk, shuffling arrest reports. Twelve people had been arrested on Friday and Saturday nights, most for fistfights and scuffles in or outside bars. His team of Larrys had made the arrests, processed the paperwork, and released the offenders, giving them a stack of related papers and a court date.

Grave's job, apparently, was to review them, initial them, and place them in an out-box marked "Larry." That process took exactly six minutes, leaving him with nothing to do the remainder of the day.

His drone, Barry, buzzed over to him. "Do we have to stay here?"

"Yes, I have to do my acting captain thingy."

"And that's just sitting? Here? All day?"

Grave shook his head. "I'll make a note of your frustration for the record."

"No, I'm serious," said Barry. "A captain is *in charge*. He can do *anything* he wants."

Grave raised an eyebrow. "You have a point. I guess we could go out, maybe get a donut. Yes, maybe talk to Wanda."

"Wanda? Who's Wanda?"

"The salesperson at Skunk 'n Donuts. She saw Ann and Grace talking."

"Perfect," said Barry. "And it's job related."

Grave slammed a hand down on the desk. "By gosh, let's do it."

Barry buzzed around the office in delight. "Yes, yes, yes."

"Whoa, whoa, whoa, little fella. First I want to go to the Crab Cove Cinema Cemetery. Talk to Victoria. See if Grace or Ann has arrived yet."

Barry slowed to a glum hover. "There gonna put you away if you keep talking to yourself at that damn cemetery."

Grave chuckled. "Well, I'm sorry your sensors can't pick her up. She's a real delight."

Barry sighed. "All right, all right, talk to no one if you must. I'll buzz around to the new graves, see if they've come up with any innovations beyond holograms and life videos."

The Crab Cove Cinema Cemetery was always coming up with something new. You could live on through professionally crafted videos or in holograms showing you at work. Grave had even heard rumors that there was going to be some new kind of simulation where your visitors could ask you questions and get an answer from the long-dead you, just as you might have answered in life. It was all a bit creepy.

Grave smiled at him. "That's the spirit. Come on, let's get out of here."

21

Rippley took a deep breath and motioned Polk to pull back the sheet on Victim Two, who was as expected completely invisible. Charlize, Smithers, and June stood to the side, watching intently.

"Can you bring her back?" said Polk, quickly adding, "I mean from, you know, invisibility, not—"

"*Death?* No, I don't have that skill, but I'll try to make her visible as best I can."

She moved her hands to where she thought the victim's head was and dropped into a deep trance, whispering at the lifeless form, repeating the words again and again without effect. She withdrew her hands. "This is a tough one."

"Do you need a break, honey?" said June. "Maybe get a soda or something?"

Rippley shook her head.

"Take your time," said Charlize.

Rippley put a finger to her lips. "Let me think, let me think. Ah!"

She moved to the other side of the slab. "I was on the wrong side. Silly."

She put her hands on the victim once more, and the body immediately started to become visible, revealing a beautiful young woman with blond hair. She was dressed in her work uniform, which consisted of black slacks and a white polo shirt sporting the logo of Vac-o-Mac, one of the leading robotic vacuum cleaner retailers. Their store was right next to Skunk 'n Donuts, on the west side of the square along Main Street.

Rippley withdrew her hands and placed them over her face, her whole body shaking. "It's Ann."

Charlize stepped up to the slab and began inspecting the body, particularly the stab wounds. "Polk, take a look at this."

Jeremy Polk stepped up on a small platform he used to make himself tall enough to view the body from above and snapped on examination gloves. "I'm not sure," he said at last. "I mean, the wounds are consistent with a large knife, even a Bowie knife, but there are far more wounds than we usually see with a Clink victim."

"I was thinking the same thing," said Charlize. "Still, I don't think we can rule him out."

"No, of course not. I'll put her through the ME-4350 Forensic Analyzer Array, and we'll see what we see."

"Right, right. How long will that take?"

Polk waggled his head, trying to come up with an estimate. "A couple of hours, perhaps longer. I want to use the slow settings so I don't miss a thing, particularly as it relates to these wounds."

"Okay," said Charlize. "Smithers-Watson and I will take June and Rippley home, then pay a visit to Vac-o-Mac to see if we can trace Ann's last steps."

Polk nodded. "Come back at five. I'm sure I'll have more information for you then."

He turned to Rippley. "Thank you again, Rippley. You've been very brave."

Rippley sniffled, then wiped her eyes. "We'll find the person who did this, won't we?"

Charlize wasn't so sure when it came to the elusive Chester Clink. "Yes, of course we will. Of course we will."

22

Loblolly and Officer Larry, who would be Detective Somebody Else tomorrow, drove in silence, at great speed, with Loblolly at the wheel of one of the few remaining "driver-activated" hovercruisers in the department's fleet of vehicles.

Snoot would have wondered at the speed, which was unusually high even for Loblolly, and deduced that something must have been troubling her. Snoot would have pressed her and gotten an answer, but Larry was new to all this, particularly extended close contact with a human, so he couldn't have guessed that what had her seething—and accelerating—was that she wasn't working directly with Grave on this case.

She thought there was a thing developing between the two of them, but maybe she was mistaken. His sidelong glances at her, his obvious nervousness in her presence, and the way his eyes met hers, lingering perhaps too long—*shit*, it all said he was at least crushing on her. Or did it? Maybe she was totally wrong about the whole thing. Maybe he even disliked her.

She pressed the pedal to the metal, causing Officer Larry to break the silence. "A hundred miles an hour seems excessive for this thirty-miles-an-hour zone, or am I missing something?"

Loblolly broke from her reverie, looked down at the gauges, and eased back on the accelerator, finally tapping on the brakes to slow their headlong rush through downtown crab cove. "Thanks, I was thinking about the case."

Officer Larry brightened. "So was I. Isn't it wonderful?"

"What?"

"The case. We're working on the case. I've never worked on one, and so far it is absolutely thrilling."

Loblolly chuckled. What a strange simdroid. "We've only been driving in this hovercruiser, Larry."

"I know, I know, but it's my first case, so I'm, I'm—"

"Excited?"

"Yes, don't you feel it, too?"

She was feeling anything but. "Yes, of course, but some advice."

"Yes?"

"Ratchet your excitement levels down a notch or two. We're talking about a murder. What I need from you, partner, is a higher level of seriousness."

Larry blinked. Perhaps she was right. "Adjusting now," he said, closing his eyes and focusing on his internal settings. "There, that should do it. I've readjusted my excitement and seriousness settings to meet your parameters. If I fail to perform up to your expectations, please advise."

Loblolly raised her eyebrows and focused back on the road. "Thank you, I will."

They drove down Main Street past the town square, turning right on Blue Crab Boulevard.

"It should only be another couple of minutes," said Loblolly. "What's that address again?"

Larry picked up the restraining order and flipped through its pages. "17784 Blue Crab Boulevard." He glanced out the window. "Looks like we're in the four hundred block."

"Farther out than I thought."

Larry looked at the hovercruiser's array of gauges. "Ten minutes at our current speed—if the traffic lights are with us."

"Right," said Loblolly.

They drove on in silence as the house numbers grew—five hundred block, six hundred block, seven hundred block—but then Larry broke the silence.

"What do you think of Mark Twain?"

Loblolly gave him an odd look. "What? What are you talking about?"

"My name. Acting Chief Grave says I have to have a new name, one that sets me apart from the other Larrys on the force."

Loblolly chuckled. "And you think Mark Twain is the way to go? Seriously?"

Larry was crestfallen. "So you don't like it?"

"No, no, he's a fine author that Mark Twain, but, um, maybe you should go with something original. I guarantee you, if you go with Mark Twain, people will start calling you Huckleberry."

Larry frowned. "Huckleberry? Really?"

Loblolly nodded. "And I'd be the first."

23

Gospel music seemed just the right thing for a cemetery, so after Grave pulled into a parking spot, he let the radio blast away until the chorus had finished their song. Then he turned off the ignition and began tapping on Barry to get his attention. Whenever Barry rode in the car, he invariably turned on his sound and vibration dampeners, so he could continue to detect incoming calls. And he had one coming in right now.

"It's Charlize," said Barry, "or rather a message from her. They've identified the second body as one Ann Aesthesia. Charlize will drop off June and Rippley at their home and then proceed to the Vac-o-Mac, the young victim's place of employment."

"Good," said Grave. "She and Grace knew each other, so the murders are most probably connected." He thought about what Wanda had told him, their argument on the night of Grace's murder.

"Shall I send an acknowledgment?"

"Yes, tell her when she's finished at Vac-o-Mac to interview Wanda Perkins at Skunk 'n Donuts. She witnessed the argument between Grace and Ann and might have more insights about their relationship."

"Very well, sir."

"Oh, and have her pick up two dozen donuts for tomorrow morning's meeting."

"Right."

Barry activated his rotors and lifted into the air just above the car. "I'm going to check out the new areas of the cemetery while you talk to yourself on that bench up the hill."

Grave shook his head. "I'll be talking to Victoria Skunkford, and you know it."

"I know no such thing, but enjoy your, um, conversation." He tilted his rotors forward and shot away up the path to the new section, leaving Grave to extricate his large frame from the small cockpit of the Sprite.

Victoria's bench was just a short walk away, and he couldn't help smiling when he spotted the ten-years-old-forever little girl in the gingham dress. Grave didn't know why he was able to see her when others couldn't, but he was genuinely happy that he could.

He greeted her long before he reached her. "Good afternoon, Victoria."

She turned and smiled at him. "Detective Grave, how wonderful to see you again. It's been quite a while, so I'm guessing you're here about another murder."

He walked up to the bench and sat down beside her. "You know me too well."

Her smile broadened. "You're all business, so it's easy to guess what you're up to. So, which new arrival are you looking for?"

Grave sighed. "Two actually."

"Two? My goodness."

"Yes, two young women, both beautiful, a blonde and a redhead."

"Hmmm."

"Oh, and both were invisible when they died."

Victoria's eyes widened. "Now it all makes sense."

"What?"

"The voices I've been hearing. Two women, one with the sweetest voice you can imagine and the other who just screams obscenities, and so shrill." She shuddered. "Awful."

"Well, I'm not sure which is which, but the women I'm looking for are named Ann Aesthesia and Grace Gnote."

"Interesting. They're both in orientation as you could probably guess. Honestly, we didn't know what else to do with them. They were just voices."

"We've managed to bring their bodies back to visibility. Do you think they'll eventually appear in the dead flesh here?"

Victoria shrugged. "Your guess is as good as mine."

"Anyway, did their voices tell you anything about their deaths?"

Victoria shook her head. "Not yet. All they've been doing is arguing. A lot of I-told-you-sos, if you know what I mean."

"I wish I did. I know they had an argument shortly before Grace's death, but I don't know what it was about."

Victoria sighed. "I'll see what I can find out, if anything."

"I'd appreciate that, Victoria."

She stood and looked down at him. "I have a few things to do now. Come back in a day or two. Perhaps I'll have something for you then."

"Yes, of course."

"Well, then, I must go now. Be sure to visit the reverend's gravesite on your way out. His parishioners have added a new feature, and the reverend is none too happy about it."

"Oh, what kind of feature?"

She shook her head. "I'm not sure what to call it, so I think you should ask the reverend about it."

And with that she disappeared.

Grave stood up and made his way back down the path towards the parking lot, then made a right, taking the much wider path to the new section of the cemetery. As he crested the hill that led down to Reverend Bendigo Bottoms' grave, he could see an unusually large crowd gathered around what looked like a bust of the reverend that had been placed on top of his tombstone.

The ghost of the reverend, who was standing apart from the crowd looking none too happy, motioned Grave over. "Simon, Simon, just the person I need."

"Hi, reverend. What's with the crowd?"

Everyone in the crowd suddenly began laughing.

The reverend shook his head, downcast. "Oh, Simon, they've gone and done it this time."

"Done what?"

The reverend flapped his arms. "I don't know who put them up to this—probably the damned cemetery director—but they've gone and created a chatbot out of me."

"A what?"

"Yeah, I said the same thing. It's a simdroid talking head that's been made to look and speak like me."

"So what's the problem?"

"So, they've gathered images, voice data, social media posts, electronic messages, and written letters by me to create a simulation specific to my personality. You can ask it questions, converse with it."

"Wow, sounds pretty cool to me, and certainly gives new meaning to the word *headstone*. So, even though you're dead, you—or rather the head—can talk with loved ones, give advice, even offer up new sermons."

The reverend shook his head. "That would be fine if it was *me* giving the advice and sermons, but this—this *thing*—is not like me at all. Oh, he sounds like me, and his facial expressions are just like mine, but the things he says."

"Like what?"

The reverend thought for a moment. "Simon, do you remember our discussions about life, death, and love?"

"Yes, of course. Life is like a tuna fish sandwich, Death is quite the entrée, and Love is like a chocolate donut."

"Exactly."

"So, what's your point?"

"Go on, go over there and ask sim-me about the meaning of life."

Grave shrugged. "All right." He made his way through the crowd and waited his turn to ask the question. The likeness to the reverend was uncanny, right down to his expressions, the tone of his voice, his word choices—even his emotions.

And now it was Grave's turn. He stepped in front of the sim-reverend and asked, "What is the meaning of life, reverend?"

The sim-reverend cocked his head. "Simon, good to see you again."

"Good to see you, too."

"The answer to your question is one I've pondered for years, and this is it: life is like a pineapple pizza."

Grave blinked.

"And what about Death, reverend?"

The sim-reverend chuckled. "I don't know much about that, but I've always thought death would be like a Sunday drive on a hovercycle. You know, a fun ride."

Grave's mouth dropped open. "Um, and what about Love?"

"My, you're full of questions today. Okay, let me see, I would have to say that love is like a sore tooth."

"I see, I see," said Grave, turning to go.

The sim-reverend called after him. "Oh, Simon, don't go. I'm about to give my new sermon on the importance of swim fins as they relate to table manners."

"Great, great," said Simon. "Can't wait."

He walked back through the crowd to the real but dead reverend, who was pacing back and forth, wringing his hands.

"I see what you mean," said Grave.

"It's a disaster, a disaster."

"It is."

"And what's worse, my parishioners and listeners are fine with all the nonsense that comes out of its mouth. Not good, Simon, not good at all. Oh, Simon, what are we going to do?"

"We?"

"Yes, we," said the reverend, "meaning you. I'm dead, what can I do? I can't pull the plug. I can't knock the thing over and smash it. And I can't talk to the cemetery director to pull it from my gravesite. Simon, Simon, Simon, I need your help." He went down on one knee and looked up at Simon. "Please."

Grave rolled his eyes. What was he getting himself into now? A little voice inside him screamed for him not to open his mouth, but his mouth had other ideas. "Okay, I'll see what I can do."

24

The sales manager at Vac-o-Mac was not being very helpful. Yes, Ann had worked there, but only for the past four weeks. And no, he had no idea if she was troubled about anything or was friends with Grace.

"I have to keep my eye on six sales associates at once, so getting to know them—any of them—is not a priority. My priority, as you might deduce, is sales. Sales pure and simple."

"Okay," said Charlize. "When was the last time you saw her?"

He flipped open a little notebook and flipped through the pages. "She last worked a Saturday shift, so that would mean she left the store about eight or thereabouts."

Charlize looked around the store, which was filled with aisle after aisle of robotic vacuum cleaners and other robotic equipment "for the modern household."

The manager watched her scan the store. "Can I interest you in a vacuum cleaner?"

"No, I was just looking around. Do you have security cameras?"

He seemed delighted. "We do, and I thought that's what you were looking for. You don't see them, do you?"

"Nope."

"My invention, actually. The lens is hair-thin, so there's no way for you to detect them. In fact, if you check your records down at the station, you'll see that we've turned in more than a few shoplifters."

Charlize nodded. "Right, well, we're going to need the footage for Saturday as part of our investigation." She had a second thought. "No, wait, we'll need the footage for Friday as well."

The manager sighed. "Very well. I'll just go get that for you."

"Good."

He began walking away but then stopped and pointed at a device floating near the ceiling. "While I'm gone, you might consider our latest product, The Gamma 500 Ceiling Duster."

Charlize nodded. "Yes, I'll have a look."

The manager walked to the back of the store and disappeared through an "employees only" doorway.

Charlize turned to Smithers-Watson. "What do you think?"

Smithers-Watson shrugged. "Unless there's something on the CCTV tapes, this has pretty much been a waste of time."

"Agreed. Okay, next stop Skunk 'n Donuts. Grave wants a couple dozen for tomorrow's meeting."

Smithers looked confused. "I thought we were going back to the morgue."

"No, I received a data transmission from Polk while we were talking to the manager. He's having problems with the analyzer. Says he'll have more information tomorrow."

"At the meeting?"

"Yes."

"So we're pretty much done for the day?"

Charlize saw the manager heading back in their direction. "No, we're going to head back to the station and review these tapes."

25

Detective Loblolly pulled the car over and parked outside Cliff Gnote's house, one of the older stilt houses near the shore and the last one on the street, just a hundred yards from the crashing waves. Even on stilts the home wouldn't last another ten years.

"This is it," she said, motioning Larry and her drone, Pine Cone, out of the vehicle. "Pine cone, do a three-sixty."

Pine Cone shot out of the vehicle and rose in the sky to survey the home.

Larry stepped out of the hovercruiser and looked up at the building. "I've heard of these but never seen one. It seems at once a good idea and an irrational defiance of global warming."

Loblolly grunted. "I guess."

Pine Cone returned and hovered between them. "Looks like no one is home."

Loblolly nodded and looked around. "No vehicle. We might have a runner."

"Shall I call it in?" said Pine Cone.

"Not yet. Let's get some eyes on the situation first." She turned to Larry. "Okay, let's head up the staircase."

"Will we need weapons?"

Loblolly considered it. Gnote was clearly a prime suspect and had a history of violence against women. "Well, he's probably not home, but are you packing?"

Larry nodded. "Of course, a Glock Laserex 99, standard issue for all Officer Larrys."

"Good, but follow my lead. This is just supposed to be a preliminary interview."

Larry nodded. "Okay, let's go."

They went up the steps to a landing and deck that wrapped around the entire house, a one-floor glass and steel boxlike home that offered uninterrupted views of the ocean and the city. And it was immediately obvious that Pine Cone was right—no one was at home. Cliff had chosen not to have curtains, so the whole interior was visible from the outside. The home was dark, not a single light on, but there was still enough available light to see that Cliff Gnote was not exactly a proponent of housekeeping.

A sleek sofa was topped with sweatshirts and other clothing, and the coffee table in front of it was a riot of beer bottles and pizza boxes. Loblolly checked the front door, but it was locked.

"Larry, you go left, I'll go right. Pine Cone, with me. Let's see if there's another way in."

They walked around the home. There were other ways in, sets of patio doors centered on each wall of the home, but they were all locked. All they could see was further evidence of a life lived without order: a sink filled with dishes, an unmade bed, and floors strewn with papers. In short, an homage to clutter.

They met again halfway around the house.

"Nothing," said Larry.

"Right," said Loblolly.

"Shall I call it in?" said Pine Cone.

Loblolly sighed. "Yes, let's not take any chances. Pine Cone, we're going to need an APB on his vehicle and a stop-fly at the airport and the Mars Terminal."

"Right," said Pine Cone. The little drone flew straight up to get the best reception.

Loblolly turned to Larry. "I guess that's it for today. Can I drop you off somewhere or do you want to go back to the station?"

"You can drop me off at the Larry Lodge."

Loblolly blinked. The Larry Lodge was really nothing more than a charging station for simdroid officers. "Okay, but now that you're a detective, you may want to consider a house of your own. The job comes with a credit increase, so you could even afford something like this house here."

Larry looked back at Cliff's house. "Really? I hadn't thought of that." He sighed.

"What?"

"Now I need a new name, new clothes, *and* a new house. I didn't think being a detective would require so much change."

"So, shall I drop you off at Larry Lodge?"

"No, you know what? Leave me here. I want to sit on the beach a while, think about all of this."

Loblolly shrugged. "Are you sure?"

"Yes, go on, I'll get a hovercab when I'm ready to go."

"Okay, then." She looked up at Pine Cone, who was descending after finishing his call to the station. "One more call, Pine Cone. Give Snoot a jingle and have her meet me at Le Crabe Bleu at six."

Pine Cone slowed his descent, then rose up again to transmission altitude.

Loblolly turned to Larry. "See you in the morning. Can't wait to see your new clothes and hear your new name."

Larry nodded and started walking to the beach.

Loblolly called after him. "But not Mark Twain, all right?"

Larry kept walking.

Loblolly shouted again. "All right, then, see you tomorrow, Huckleberry."

Larry stopped and looked back at her. "Don't call me Huckleberry."

Loblolly laughed. "Then come up with a great name."

Larry nodded and walked on, wondering how many hours he'd have to spend on the beach to come up with anything that would prevent a Huckleberry response from Loblolly.

Being a detective was a strange business.

26

Grave began groaning as soon as he saw the lighthouse parking lot. Ida Notion's new car, a Tesla Muskox Flyer, was sitting there in all its red-winged glory, as it did each and every Sunday evening. Their Sunday family get-together was a long-standing tradition, and Grave, faced with two murders and new responsibilities, had completely forgotten about it.

He checked his watch. Quarter to six. He was more than an hour late.

"This is not going to go well," he said.

Barry whirred to life. "Sir?"

"Nothing, Barry. It's just that I'm late for Sunday dinner."

"No worries, sir. Roderick will have worked them through a fine array of appetizers and wines, I'm sure."

Grave wasn't so sure. Roderick didn't like surprises. Yes, he was fully capable of handling Sunday dinner, but he'd never been faced with an hour alone with Ida and Grave's father, Jacob. Grave wasn't sure *anyone* could handle ten minutes of that, let alone an hour. "Okay, we'll just have to hope for the best. Come on, let's go."

He had expected dead quiet when he opened the lighthouse door, but instead he and Barry were met with raucous laughter coming from the living room level. Grave climbed slowly up the spiral staircase, the laughter growing in volume with each step. And then he caught sight of them. Ida and Jacob were sitting on the sofa, laughing, with Horace on the floor in front of them, waving his wings this way and that.

"And then," said Horace, "and then I took the french-fry right out of the man's mouth."

Ida and Jacob burst into laughter again, then spotted Grave.

"Oh, my word, Simon," said Ida, "come in, come in. Horace has been regaling us with story after story. You never told us he was so droll."

Grave raised a brow and looked down at Horace. "I didn't know he was."

Horace cocked his head and lifted his wings. "Just passing the time, waiting for you."

Grave sighed and turned to his father. "Sorry I'm late."

Jacob Grave nodded. "The two murders, right?"

Grave gave Ida a look. "So you picked up on that?"

Ida nodded. "The second one was invisible, too, right?"

"Yes, very much so."

"Two women."

"Yes."

Ida turned to Jacob. "I told you so."

Jacob Grave shrugged. "I never doubted you, Ida, but you know, I still find it a bit freaky, your abilities."

Ida looked at Simon and rolled her eyes. "This man, what am I gonna do with him."

Jacob looked at his watch. "Feed him dinner, I hope."

"Speaking of which," said Simon. "Where's Roderick?"

"In the kitchen, doing his thing," said Horace.

"Right," said Grave. "I'll just go have a word with him."

He went back to the stairs and climbed up to the kitchen level. Roderick had the Surround Vision on, watching *Casablanca*. It looked like he was sitting on a stool in Rick's Cafe. Bogart looked slightly drunk and was beginning another famous line: "Of all the gin-joints . . ."

Grave cleared his throat. "Roderick."

Roderick startled and turned off the Surround Vision. "Oh, you're here at last."

"Is everything okay? You look a bit frazzled."

Roderick nodded. "Your father and that, um, woman."

"How long did you last?"

"About seven minutes, then I had to excuse myself. They're quite a pair."

"*Insufferable* is the word you're looking for."

Roderick chuckled. "That would work."

Grave looked around and saw no sign of dinner. "So where do we stand on dinner?"

Roderick sighed. "The fish may be a little dry, but I think we'll be fine. I just need a few minutes to pull it all together."

Grave nodded. "Good, I'll just go up top and watch the sunset."

"Would you like wine with your sunset?"

Grave smiled. "Good idea."

"Go on up, I'll bring you a glass shortly."

"Make it *tall*-ly."

When he reached the observation deck, the sun was putting on another grand finale, the sky a kaleidoscopic swirl of yellows, oranges, reds, and purples.

A few miles away on a lonely beach, Officer Larry was watching the same sunset. And then it came to him. *A name!*

27

Detective Loblolly prevented any conversation about her so-called *relationship* with Grave by launching a preemptive finger in the air. "No, Amanda, we will not be discussing that, not here, not anywhere."

"But," said Detective Snoot before the admonishing finger had shut her down completely. She sighed. "As you wish."

"Now," said Loblolly, "I want to hear everything about this first meeting of the recruitment team." She looked around at the other tables, searching for their waiter. "Assuming we can at least get our drinks."

Le Crabe Bleu, arguably the most expensive restaurant in Crab Cove, was packed, and Loblolly could see a line of people waiting for tables. The noise level was high, as usual, even though it was an outdoor café. A hundred personal drones hovered above them, most noisy old models on their last rotors. Diners valiantly tried to hold conversations by raising their voices and leaning across the tables.

She spotted the waiter walking toward them with a tray containing what looked like their drinks. "Ah, here he is."

The waiter placed the Old Bay Martinis in front of them with a flourish. "Mademoiselles."

"Thank you, Maurice," said Loblolly. "Kind of crowded tonight so we'll have a second round whenever you can get to it."

The waiter scraped a crumb off the table, turned, and marched away.

"He's kind of cute," said Snoot. "Don't you think?"

Loblolly rolled her eyes. "No talking about men tonight, unless we're talking about the men at your meeting."

Snoot took a sip of the drink, which was really nothing more than a standard vodka martini with a sprinkle of Old Bay Seasoning on top and a celery curl garnish. She plucked the garnish out and popped it in her mouth. "I'm famished."

Loblolly followed her lead. "This is just what I need."

"So," said Snoot, growing serious. "The meeting."

"Right, go on."

Snoot took a deep breath and launched in. The recruitment team consisted of herself, three city council members, a human resources professional, and an outside consultant-headhunter from Cove Recruitment. They had all seemed surprised that Snoot was included on the team, and they tried to talk around her during the first few minutes of the meeting. Finally, Snoot had had enough and inserted herself into the discussion, pointing out that she knew more about the Police Chief job than any of them did.

"The job description sucked," said Snoot, "so we spent most of the meeting rewriting the *real* requirements for the job."

That process had taken more than two hours. They had then turned to questions of process, from the review of resumes, to the number and manner of interviews that would be involved, and who would act as interviewers.

"It was exhausting, but in the end and despite their objections, I'll be conducting the initial screenings of the external candidates. Then all of us will interview the internal and external candidates and try to reach consensus."

Loblolly had been nodding like a bobble-head as Snoot explained the process and kept bobbling a few seconds after Snoot had finished. "Sounds good. So, are there internal candidates?"

Snoot wagged a finger at her. "Sorry, I can't share that."

Loblolly smiled. "Ooh, aren't we being official."

Snoot chuckled. "I'd tell you if I could."

"No, no, that's fine." Loblolly raised her glass. "To the process."

Snoot clinked her glass against Loblolly's. "The process." She took a quick sip, then set her glass down. Her sigh seemed to ripple through the restaurant.

"What?"

"Captain Morgan. He didn't retire. He was forced out by the mayor."

Loblolly set her glass down. "What the—"

"Yeah, I know. It sucks."

Loblolly sat back in her chair and began drumming her fingers on the table. "We can't let this stand."

"I don't think we have much of a choice. It's done. Morgan has emptied his office and is pretty much gone."

Now it was Loblolly's turn to sigh. "It's just not freakin' right."

Snoot shook her head, then picked up her glass. "To Captain Morgan."

Loblolly lifted her glass in solemn toast. "Captain Morgan."

They sipped at their martinis and grew silent. Snoot looked at her watch. "Where's our food?"

Loblolly looked around, but there was no waiter in sight. "I think I may have lost my appetite." She lifted her glass to take another sip.

Snoot tried to change the subject. "So, how's your new partner?"

Loblolly's laugh burst from her, a fine spray of martini reaching Snoot on the other side of the table.

Snoot picked up her napkin and began wiping her face. "Well, thank you."

Loblolly continued laughing. "Sorry, sorry, but it was quite a day."

"Why so funny? What did he do?"

Loblolly wiped her eyes. "Oh, my. It wasn't anything he did. He seems capable enough. And he's so sweet."

"Then what?"

"Simon gave him an order, and he's having trouble with it." She began to giggle.

"Come on, out with it." She couldn't help giggling herself.

"So, Simon told him to ditch his uniform by tomorrow and have a new name, so we could distinguish him from all the other Officer Larrys."

Snoot nodded. "Makes sense to me. So what's so funny?"

Loblolly's giggle worked its way up to a snicker and then jumped to a snort. "The first name he came up with was Mark Twain."

Snoot raised an eyebrow. "So? How is that funny? He's a great writer."

"Yeah, yeah, I know that, but I told him if he did that, everyone would start calling him Huckleberry."

"Okay, I'm not getting this at all. How is that funny?"

Loblolly sighed. "You had to be there. The look on his face. He was just, um, crestfallen, you know, but in a comical way."

Snoot shook her head. "You're a strange woman, you know that?"

"No, seriously, if you could have seen his face, you'd be laughing, too."

Snoot cocked her head. "Maybe. Anyway, I'll have to take your word for it. So, does he have another name in mind?"

"He didn't when I left him."

"I guess we'll just have to be surprised in the morning."

"Yeah."

Snoot lifted her glass. "Okay, a toast to whatever he calls himself."

"To Huckleberry!"

28

Grave delayed the Monday morning meeting as long as he could, but once the donuts ran out—without him getting a single one, as usual—the team seemed to grow restless.

"Can't we get this going?" said Polk. "I have work to do back at the morgue."

"Yes, of course. I was waiting for Officer Larry to show up, but apparently he's going to be a no-show." He walked to the center of the squad room. "Okay, folks, everyone who's working on the town square murders to the conference room, please."

Everyone stopped their side conversations and shuffled into the conference room, trailed by Polk and Grave.

Grave waited until they were all seated, then turned to Polk. "Jeremy, why don't you start things off? What do we know?"

Polk cleared his throat, puffed out his chest, and began pacing back and forth at the head of the conference table, raising a finger in the air to make each point. "Two murders, both young women, both invisible, both killed within an hour of each other on Friday night."

The last point was a surprise. "Wait," said Grave. "Both on Friday night?"

"Yes, one in the square and one elsewhere."

Charlize raised a hand. "So he kept the body for almost twenty-four hours before depositing it back in the square?"

"So it seems," said Polk.

Charlize frowned. "That's not like our Chester Clink."

"No, it isn't," said Smithers-Watson.

Polk held up a hand. "Hold your fire a second. Charlize, you are absolutely correct. It's not like him at all, and neither are the knife wounds on the second victim. Not like his at all. They seemed purposeful enough, but they were more random than we would expect from Chester Clink."

"A copycat, then," said Grave.

Polk shrugged. "Not a very good copycat if that's what we're dealing with."

Loblolly raised a hand. "If I may, sir. I think we're forgetting that the victim was invisible. Even Chester Clink wouldn't have experience killing an invisible woman. What we think of as random stabs may be the result of her invisibility."

"He didn't know exactly where she was," said Grave.

"Exactly," said Loblolly. "So his signature was all wrong."

"Yes, yes that could be. What do you think, Polk?"

Polk had been nodding his head the whole time. He knew it was possible. "The angles of the wounds would suggest just that."

"All right," said Grave. "We won't rule Clink out."

"It's still puzzling, though," said Charlize. "He kills the first one, leaving her in the square, but for some reason kills the second one— using a different method, mind—and then brings her back to the square the next night."

"I agree," said Grave. "It's odd."

"Maybe we're talking about two killers," said Loblolly.

Grave cocked his head. "I suppose that's possible, but what are the odds that two invisible women would be murdered on the same night by two different murderers?"

"Stranger things have happened," said Charlize, "so I think we have to be open to that."

Grave nodded, then turned back to Loblolly. "Speaking of possibilities, any luck finding Cliff Gnote?"

Loblolly frowned. "No. He wasn't at home, and we haven't been able to trace his car or his drone—must be using a detection blocker.

And so far, no luck at the airport, the bus terminal, or the Mars Terminal. He's vanished."

"All right," said Grave. "Keep after him, and let me know if you make any progress."

"Yes, sir."

Grave looked at the door, hoping to see Officer Larry coming in, but there was no Larry. "All right, let's proceed to next steps. Charlize, if you don't mind, the Surround Vision."

Charlize picked up the controller and punched in a code, the conference room transforming into a miniature view of the town square on Friday night. "Here we go."

Grave had to chuckle. They all looked like giants in this Surround Vision display. He could walk across the square in two strides. "Each of you will have assignments tonight when we walk through a one-for-one display of the scene of Friday night."

He turned to Charlize. "First things first, Charlize. We know that the two women had a heated conversation here at Skunk 'n Donuts. I'd like you and Smithers to be flies on the wall for that conversation. There's no sound, of course, so you'll need to take someone who can read lips."

Smithers-Watson raised his hand. "I can do that, sir."

"Really?"

"Yes, it came in very handy when I was a butler at the Hawthorne Mansion."

Grave nodded. "Okay, great. We'll need a complete transcript of what was said."

He turned away from Skunk 'n Donuts and took a step into the square. "Now, Grace worked at Skunk 'n Donuts, and Ann worked one door down, at Vac-o-Mac. To reach their hovercruisers at the parking lot on the east side of the square, they would have had to take this sidewalk here on the west side, on Main Street. Then they would have proceeded to and around the gazebo, passing the chess players as they went, and then taken this diagonal path to the parking lot on the corner of Blue Crab Boulevard and Imperial Avenue. And, of course, the bodies were found here and here, just yards apart."

Charlize interrupted. "So victim one didn't reach the parking lot. Her cruiser should still be there, then."

"Yes," said Grave. "We'll have to check that out."

"And the second victim would have been brought back to the square Saturday night by someone who parked there. The Surround Vision should show that."

"Exactly," said Grave, looking at his watch. "Okay, we have a full day before tonight's work at the stadium." He turned to Charlize. "I'd like you and Smithers-Watson to thoroughly familiarize yourselves with the town square and all the buildings surrounding it. I think that knowledge will help us as we view the square in the dark."

"Yes, sir," said Charlize, and if I may, I'd like to check out that parking lot and talk to the chess players, if they're there."

Grave nodded. "Exactly what I was about to say." He turned to Loblolly and handed her an envelope. "Here's a warrant on the Cliff Gnote home. Check out the interior to see if you can find anything that will help us find him. Take as many Larrys as you want."

"Yes, sir."

"Speaking of which, I don't suppose you know where our Officer Larry is. It's not like him to be late."

She shook her head. "Haven't had a word from him since last night. He was struggling to come up with a name and appropriate clothing. Maybe he's shopping. Dunno."

"Well, when he shows up, I'll send him out there to help you." He looked around the room. "Oh, one more thing. Loblolly, did the student forms mention next of kin?"

Loblolly pulled out the two folders and flipped each open in turn. "No and no."

"Okay, I'll follow up with June and Rippley. Perhaps they know more." He turned to Charlize. "And you might ask their employers if they know anything. The press is going to sniff this out and I'd rather have that information before we give them anything more about the cases."

"Their employers weren't helpful at all, but to your point, how should we respond to the press if we're asked?"

"Refer them all to me. Say nothing more."

Everyone nodded. "Okay, then. I'll see you all at the stadium just before sunset."

As they all began to leave, the door to the conference room burst open and a Morgan Freeman simdroid walked in. He wore white cotton slacks and a matching collarless shirt, the kind of shirt you'd find in India. Unlike Officer Larry, this Morgan Freeman had a short grizzled beard. His smile was serene.

"Officer Larry?" said Grave.

The man shook his head. "Not anymore, sir. The name is God."

Grave blinked, hard, and then everyone laughed.

29

The leaves on the trees that lined the Fourth Coastal Highway shook as Grave and his Sprite passed by, Gospel music pegged at eleven creating what looked like a green wave in the car's wake. Grave paid no attention to the trees or the music. He was alternately chuckling about Officer Larry's decision and worrying about the cases.

Larry, aka God, had reviewed Morgan Freeman's filmography and settled on the God character in *Bruce Almighty*. Grave did his best to explain that it wouldn't reflect well on him if he went around calling himself God. Everyone would think he was insane. Larry didn't see the problem, but promised to call himself Larry the rest of the day, unless he came up with a better name.

There was nothing amusing about the cases, and they were both puzzling. They had to be connected, at least in Grave's mind, but the different manners of death—a snapped neck as opposed to multiple stab wounds—suggested two killers. He also wondered why Ann was killed elsewhere and then dumped in the town square the next night. It didn't make sense.

He pulled the Sprite over in front of the Blunt home and turned off the ignition. The gospel music stopped, but Barry filled the silence immediately. "Sir, you've had two calls."

"Go on."

"Mayor Change wants to see you in his office immediately, and there was also a call from that reporter woman, Claire Fairly."

If there was such a thing as a double grimace, Grave did his best to emulate it. The mayor, the first simdroid elected to public office, was out for blood. He'd already pressured Morgan to retire, and the rumor in the station was that he wanted to replace all human detectives with simdroids. As for Claire Fairly, she was perhaps the most annoying and persistent reporter cum news anchor in Crab Cove and perhaps in the world. "Oh, great."

He climbed out of the car, Barry following. "Message the mayor that I'm working the case and will be at his office in an hour or so. He'll probably press for a specific time. Do not return his messages or calls. I'll get there when I get there."

"What about Ms. Fairly?"

Grave puffed out his cheeks. This was a little trickier. "For starters, don't tell her where we are or that I'll be with the mayor later today. I don't want her and her news crew surrounding town hall or Blunt's home."

"So?"

Grave pursed his lips. "Tell her I'll give her a call tomorrow morning. And again, do not reply further to her, no matter how many times she calls or messages."

"Yes, sir."

Grave started walking to the front door. "Okay, then, get to it, and when you're finished, stay outside. I won't need you in here."

"Yes, sir." Barry lifted into the air and hovered above the Sprite. He would "get to it," as instructed.

June Blunt answered the doorbell immediately, ushering him inside without a word.

"I'd like to talk with you and Rippley if you don't mind."

"Of course," said June. "I've been expecting you."

"Really?"

"You'll want to know more about Grace and Ann and their classmates, am I right?"

Grave raised an eyebrow. "Perhaps you should be a detective as well. That's exactly why I'm here, but also to see if either of you know anything about their next of kin."

June nodded. "Okay, Rippley is back in the classroom."

"Giving a class?"

"No, we've suspended all future classes for the moment. Rippley is not sure she should continue. I mean, given the murders."

"Makes sense."

They walked down the hall to the room Rippley had been using as a classroom. She was sitting behind a small desk and was no more or less visible than the cloudlike June.

"Honey," said June. "Detective Grave has a few questions for us."

She looked up, smiled in a weak and cloudy way, then became fully visible, her hair going from muted to flaming red. "Good to see you, Simon. Have you found the murderer?"

She gets right to the point, thought Grave. "Not yet, but I promise you we'll find him."

She nodded. "You say you have questions?"

"Yes, basically, anything more you can tell us about Grace and Ann. For starters, are you aware of any next of kin for either of them?"

"That's an easy question, and the answer is no for both, and by that I mean no next of kin for either of them. I think that's why they immediately bonded."

"Are you sure?"

"Yes, we talked about it once after class. Both sets of parents were killed in the Crab Cove Ferry Disaster back in 2045."

"Wow, I remember that. Hundreds killed."

"That's what they said."

"Right, right. So they were in the same class?"

"Yes, even graduated the same day, just a few weeks ago."

"Okay, in your after-class talks, did the name Cliff Gnote ever come up?"

Rippley rolled her eyes. "Several times. He was a pest. Even tried to join the class. Of course, we turned him away. Our class is no place for a brute like that."

"No, of course not. But let me ask this. Were there other people in their class?"

Rippley smiled. "Good point, and yes, of course. Let me check the class lists." She pulled out a small memory tablet and tapped on its screen a few times. "Here we go. In addition to Ann and Grace, there were four other students: Jack Friendly, Malcom Spitzer, Penelope Goodlove, and Wayne John Dough—and that's D, O, U, G, H, not D, O, E."

Grave blinked at that, but it slide for the moment. *John Dough? Really?* "Did any of them interact with Ann or Grace?"

"Interact?"

"You know, behave in a friendly or not-so-friendly way with them?"

"Ah, you think they may be suspects."

Grave nodded. "It's a possibility."

"Two things, then. First, I don't remember any interactions with those other students, and second, you have the student folders, so you have all you need to follow up."

"Yes, of course, but I'd be interested in what you could tell me about each of them, apart from what may be in their student records."

"Okay, Simon, this may take a while, so you might want to take a seat." She pointed at a nearby chair, and Simon dutifully sat down. Over the next twenty minutes she tried her best to describe each of them.

Jack Friendly was a tall, thin man, age about thirty, who struggled mightily in class. The best he could do was make himself invisible from his head to his waist. His reason for wanting to become invisible was to avoid his mother-in-law. He had just recently switched to a special class for other students struggling to become fully invisible.

Malcolm Spitzer, on the other hand, was a good student and had graduated along with Grace and Ann. He was a stocky young man in his early twenties. Rippley said his most striking feature was his nose, which was long, thin, and pointed. "Almost birdlike," she had said. And that's why he had joined the class. There were just those social situations where he felt uncomfortable about his nose.

Rippley didn't think Penelope Goodlove was a likely suspect. She was just eight years old. Like Rippley, she had red hair but of a shade more rusty than flaming. She had joined the class for two reasons. First, she had a large birthmark on her face in the shape of an owl, and second and most important to her, she wanted to be a private investigator. "She thinks being invisible will have definite advantages." Grave couldn't argue with that.

When Rippley came to Wayne John Dough, Rippley beamed about how he was her best student ever. "He got it right away and often helped me with the other students. He's a natural teacher. Could easily open his own school." When she described his physical appearance, Grave felt a chill go through his entire body.

Chester Clink to a tee.

30

Charlize and Smithers had spent hours walking in and around the town square. They had talked to Wanda again and learned nothing new about Ann's and Grace's relationship or the subject of their Friday night argument. They had searched the parking lot, found Grace's hovercruiser, and had it towed to the station for a thorough once-over by the forensics team. There was no sign of Ann's hovercruiser, however. Charlize surmised that the killer had used it to transport the body to and from the murder site and then made off with it or disposed of it. A quick drive off a pier in auto-mode and it would be gone forever.

They had also spent a lot of time looking for sight angles the killer may have used to watch the victims' progress across the square before pouncing on them. Officer Larry's analysis—that the murderer had hidden just out of sight behind the curve of the gazebo—seemed to be exactly the best spot. There was a clear view and the distance from the gazebo to the victim was the shortest. It would only take a few seconds to rush from cover and overcome the victim.

Finally, they had interviewed the chess players, who were no help at all. They had been so focused on their game, they didn't notice anyone else in the square, or so they said. Charlize had given the chessboard a quick look and determined that from the positions of the chess pieces, the players were both amateurs. Charlize could have checkmated either of them in three moves.

The man playing the white pieces was Lev Korsokov, a middle-aged manager at the Crab Cove Tourist Bureau. He was bald and seemed to have no neck between his head and his broad shoulders and enormous belly. As they talked, his amber eyes darted from his opponent to the chessboard to Charlize, as if searching for someplace safe to rest.

His opponent, Dewey Ditts, a young man who worked as a member of the ground crew at the Mars Terminal, was Korsokov's physical opposite, lean and rangy, with a straw for a neck. Like Korsokov, he seemed more interested in the game than Charlize's questions.

Finally, Charlize had thanked them for their time and walked away with Smithers-Watson.

"They seemed nervous to me," said Smithers.

"Yes, I got the same feeling. Then again, they may have been overcome by my beauty, or rather the beauty of young Charlize Theron—I get that a lot."

Smithers-Watson nodded. "There's that, of course, but I sensed something more. I think they may be up to something."

Charlize turned and looked back at them. "Maybe. It will be interesting to see if they show up on the Surround Vision tonight."

"Right," he said. "Speaking of which, we should probably head on over to the stadium. Make sure everything is ready to go by dusk."

Charlize nodded. "Right. Come on, this should be fun."

31

Grave's hope of containing news of the two murders blew up the moment he pulled his Sprite into the city hall parking lot. News crews were everywhere, and all of them were heading toward him. And how could they not with the sound of gospel music rattling the windows of city hall as he arrived?

Claire Fairly was in the lead, clacking along the pavement in red heels and a tight-fitting red dress that pinched at her knees, making progress problematic. Although she was yards away, she had stretched out her microphone, hoping for any sound that might come her way. The effect was that of a woman being tugged along by the microphone, like she was walking an invisible dog. He wondered briefly whether Rippley had trained dogs to be invisible. *That* would be something.

He shook off the thought, gave the approaching Fairly a quick smile, and strode away toward the safety of the town hall. Fairly called after him, her voice pleading, but Grave just pushed through the doors and nodded at the guards, who quickly shut the door, stopping Fairly and the rest of the pressing press cold.

Grave took the elevator to the second floor and walked down a long marble corridor to the double-doored office of Mayor Lester "Les" Change. The mayor's secretary, a simdroid patterned after First Lady Nancy Reagan, rose from her desk and tried to prevent Grave from entering, but Grave just gave her a quick smile and swung open the double doors.

The mayor, the spitting image of President Ronald Reagan, looked up from a pile of papers and frowned. "Oh, it's you. About time."

Grave didn't wait for permission to sit down. He pulled back one of the visitor chairs opposite the mayor's desk and sat down. "Been a little busy."

The mayor sat back in his chair and folded his hands. "Well?"

Grave gave him a confused look. "Well what?"

"The murders, have you solved them?"

Grave blinked. "It's only been a couple of days."

The mayor rapped his knuckles on the desk. "Three days."

Grave rolled his eyes. "Yes, three days."

"And yet there's no progress."

Grave scoffed. "Of course there's progress. We're following up clues, leads. My teams are in the field as we speak, gathering information." He wondered whether to mention the likely involvement of Chester Clink, but thought better of it. No one had ever apprehended the man, including Grave, and he thought the mayor would be less than pleased.

The mayor shook his head. "Come on, that sounds like bad television."

Grave shrugged. "It's what we do, what detectives do. Murderers don't just say, 'Well, it's been three days. Guess I better turn myself in.'"

The mayor drummed his fingers on the desk, another executive mannerism that, like knuckle rapping, had been programmed in. "I knew I shouldn't have let Morgan appoint you as acting chief. You're like him. Human, therefore fallible, illogical, emotional . . ." His voice trailed off after he had apparently lost interest in additional adjectives.

"One, I didn't ask for this job. Two, one of our best simdroid detective teams is on the case. Three, I really don't give a damn if you replace me. And four, you should have never forced out Captain Morgan in the first place. I'm sure we'd have been further along with him at the helm."

The mention of Morgan had the mayor out of his seat. "Morgan is gone and *won't* be back."

Grave rose from his seat to look the mayor in the eye. "Then replace me *right now* or give me the time to work this case *my* way."

The mayor sat back down, steaming, and looked up at Grave. "I want a report on your progress by noon tomorrow, followed by a press conference later in the day. Failing that, you're done."

Grave wondered whether to take off his badge right then and there and throw it on the mayor's desk. But then he thought about his teams in the field. There was no telling what kind of acting chief the mayor might appoint and how he, she, or it might manage Grave and his fellow detectives. He had to protect them if he could.

He took a deep breath, turned on his heels, and strode for the door. "Noon, then," he said over his shoulder.

The mayor said nothing more.

32

Loblolly looked down at the trip-tracker and turned to God. "We're about halfway there."

God said nothing. Just sat there looking at the hovercruiser's computer screen.

"What are you doing?" she said.

God tapped on the screen. "Morgan Freeman's filmology. Do you know he acted in more than 140 films?"

"Nope."

"Played God a few times, not just in *Bruce Almighty*."

"You can't be God, Huckleberry."

"I know and don't call me Huckleberry."

She chuckled. "Well, you best choose *someone* to be."

God sighed. "He played Nelson Mandela in *Invictis*. How about him?"

"No, too close to godlike. We don't need that at the station."

God moved his finger down the list. "How about Eddie 'Scrap-Iron' Dupree in *Million Dollar Baby*."

"An old boxer? Um, no, not him."

The finger moved lower. "How about Ned Logan in *Unforgiven*?"

"A cowboy? No."

God sighed. "Okay, ah, here's one. How about Detective William Somerset in *Se7en*?"

Loblolly waggled her head, weighing the choice. He was good in that. "Well, you're getting closer. At least he's a detective, but that was one dark, dark movie. Who else you got?"

God looked back at the screen. "Oh, how about Lucius Fox in the Batman movies?"

Loblolly pursed her lips. "Nah, as I recall, he wore bowties. I hate bowties."

God threw up his hands. "What then?"

"I don't know, you've got the list."

God looked back at the list. "Here's one that might work. Dr. Alex Cross in *Along Came a Spider*. He played a forensic psychologist."

Loblolly raised an eyebrow. "Forensic psychologist, huh? We could use one of those. Charlize has some skills, but a real expert she's not. But can you be that?"

God nodded. "Yes, it's just a matter of programming. I can stop at the Upgrade Center tomorrow morning. No problem."

Loblolly smiled. "Okay, Alex Cross it is. Now, you'll also need new clothes. A beige trench coat, a fedora, a black vest, a few ties—nothing too flashy—and some good wool slacks."

God nodded for the last time. "Okay, just call me Alex from here on out."

"Okay, Huckleberry."

"Hey, don't call me that."

Loblolly laughed. "Okay, fine, fine. And look, we're here."

She pulled the hovercruiser into Cliff Gnote's driveway. "All right, let's go, Doc. We're losing light."

Alex smiled back at her, a simdroid on the cusp of change and becoming.

33

Victoria Skunkford could tell something was wrong the moment Grave slumped down on the bench next to her. "Are you okay?"

Grave leaned forward and put his face in his hands. "Yes, no, I don't know." He sat back up and took a deep breath. "I'll be okay."

"Simon, this isn't like you. What's going on?"

Grave shook his head, wondering whether to share the growing list with her. "It's this new job of mine as acting chief. It's just not me and now the mayor is on my case, trying to rush the investigation. I have until noon tomorrow to make progress—or else."

Victoria frowned. She had no idea how to help him, so she patted his shoulder. "There, there, Simon. I'm sure you'll rise to the occasion. Speaking of which, I have spoken to Grace and Ann about their murders."

Grave brightened. "Really?"

"Yes, they're even visible now."

"Do you think I could talk with them?"

Victoria shook her head. "I asked that very question, but they are reluctant to get involved."

"Get involved? They were murdered. You'd think they'd want to bring their killer or killers to justice."

"I thought that, too, but they are barely speaking to one another. Speaking to anyone but me is not something either wants to do, at least right now."

"I just don't understand it."

"Nor I, but you have to remember that death is a traumatic event, even if your death is a quiet one, like slipping from life in the night."

"I guess."

"And their deaths were brutal. Grace is looking in the wrong direction, and Ann is still having trouble dealing with all those knife wounds. She just keeps picking at them."

"All right, so can you please keep pursuing answers? Even knowing whether we're dealing with one killer or two would be a great help."

Victoria nodded. "I will."

Grave slumped back on the bench and looked at the sky. "So, how are things otherwise?"

Victoria shrugged. "Same old same old. New arrivals, orientations, processing, dispositions. Always a dull moment."

"I don't know how you do it year after year."

She chuckled. "Oh, Simon, it's what I do, and besides, time is different for me than for you. Past, present, future—they're meaningless for me."

Grave looked at his watch. "But not for me. Listen, I have to go. We're setting up a Surround Vision of the events at the stadium, so I best be going."

Victoria smiled. "I'll keep working on Grace and Ann. If you haven't solved the case by tomorrow morning, come back. Maybe we can beat that noon deadline you're so worried about."

Grave stood up. "Tomorrow, then. Now I have to go collect Barry. He's fascinated by this cemetery. I guess because he's just facing decommissioning or obsolescence, not death."

Victoria cocked her head. "Sounds like the same thing to me."

Grave chuckled. "I'll tell him that." Grave gave Victoria a little wave and began walking down the path. He knew where he'd find Barry, and that's exactly where he was: at the grave of the Reverend Bendigo Bottoms.

There were no crowds and no Bendigo, only the talking chatbot head atop the reverend's gravestone. Barry was hovering in front of it when he spotted Grave. "This thing is unbelievable. I hope you do this when you go, so I can continue our relationship."

Grave snorted. "As if. According to the reverend, it's pretty much a bust."

"Well, yeah, it is a bust. Just the head and shoulders."

"No, I mean it's not a fair portrayal of what the reverend was in life. It's a bit askew on his personality and reasoning."

Barry waggled in the air. "It's answered all my questions."

"Like what?"

"Oh, like the meaning of life. I've always been puzzled by the fact that I'm not considered alive. And do you know what he said?"

"That life is like a tuna fish sandwich?"

"A sandwich? No, of course not. He said that life was like a bowl of applesauce topped by diodes."

"Diodes?"

"Yes, a two-terminal semiconductor. I have several, you know, so that bit makes sense to me. I'm struggling with the applesauce part, though."

Grave nodded. "As would I." He looked at the head, which was eyeing him, no doubt waiting for Grave to ask a question. He wondered whether to bring the chatbot up to speed on the case, if only to hear bad solutions in return, but decided against it. "Come on, Barry, we have to get to the stadium."

34

Loblolly, her drone Pine Cone, and a god reborn as Detective Alex Cross had spent hours going through Cliff Gnote's house and had turned up nothing of interest. The man had apparently walked out of the house and disappeared, leaving the house in shambles and taking nothing with him. His closets were full and his suitcase was untouched.

Loblolly looked out the living room window. The sun was beginning to set. "Alex, I think we need to wrap this up. We'll be needed at the stadium."

Alex put down a box of documents he was searching through. "Right, right. Still . . ."

"What?"

"Well, we haven't checked the outside yet." He held up a document. "And this suggests he owns a boat."

"Really," said Loblolly, taking the document. "Hch, a PowerGlider 6000. How could he afford that?"

Alex shrugged. "Dunno, but there are several boats moored at a pier just a little ways down the beach."

"How do you know that?"

"After you left me here last time, I spent some time on the beach, remember?"

"Where you came up with the God idea."

"Yes, even watched the sunset."

"If I were God, I'd do the same thing." She checked her watch. "All right, let's go, a few minutes on the beach won't have us too late."

They locked the house and walked out to the beach, where they could see boats bobbing in the water next to a pier.

Alex stopped in his tracks. "No PowerGlider."

Loblolly shielded her eyes with her hand so she could get a better look. "Wait, is that it?" She pointed toward the setting sun."

"Yes, that's it."

Loblolly turned to Pine Cone. "Give chase, but don't get too close."

Pine Cone waggled in the air and then shot away, Loblolly calling after her, "And call the Coast Guard."

Pine Cone was already too far away to hear. Loblolly turned back to Alex. "I don't think she heard me. Let's get back to the cruiser and call them."

"Right," said Alex. "Better call Grave, too."

"Yes, of course."

They began running, Alex far outdistancing her as he shifted his legs into super sprint mode.

Loblolly was about to call out wait up, but as soon as she opened her mouth, she tripped and fell, sand spraying everywhere.

Alex stopped and ran back to her. "Are you okay?" He reached down to offer a helping hand, but Loblolly pulled her hand away.

"Come on, let me give you a hand."

She looked up at him. "I think not." She rose to her knees and began patting the air above the sand next to her, finally pulling it back in horror.

Alex could see the shock on her face. "What?"

"I think we've found our Mr. Gnote."

Alex pointed at the bay. "I thought he was in the boat?"

Loblolly shook her head. "I don't think so. I think he's right here on the ground—quite invisible and certainly dead."

Alex raised an eyebrow. "How do you know it's Gnote—or even a man?"

She patted the invisible body again and again. "He's the right height and has all the necessary body parts."

"Oh." He looked out at the bay. The boat and Pine Cone were out of sight. "Then who's on the boat?"

Loblolly shrugged. "I guess we'll find out." She picked up a seashell and placed it on top of the body. It seemed to hover over it. "Come on, we have a ton of calls to make."

35

Grave watched the crime scene tape flickering in the wind near the body, which continued to be invisible. Even the crime scene lights arrayed around it couldn't reveal for sure who the man was. Loblolly thought it was Gnote for sure, but Grave knew from experience not to jump too far ahead of the facts. This body could just as easily be another student. If so, Gnote was most likely heading for the open waters of the Atlantic. If not, the man in the boat might be Chester Clink.

He walked over to Polk, who was just standing up after examining the body. "What do you think, Polk?"

"Well, as Loblolly said, he's a man, all right."

"She thinks he's Cliff Gnote."

"I don't know who it is."

"Cause and time of death?"

"Too soon to say. We'll have to get Rippley Blunt to help us again." Grave checked his watch. "Probably past her bedtime."

Polk nodded. "It can wait till morning." He motioned over one of his forensic team members. "Phil, let's get the body back to the morgue."

"Yes, sir."

"But let's keep this area roped off. I want you guys to do another sweep in daylight."

Phil nodded and walked away. Polk turned back to Grave. "A dead man on the beach and someone on a boat, and apparently fleeing."

"And a missing car, don't forget that."

"So maybe yet another person involved?"

"Could be. Catching whoever's on the boat would be a great start—and identifying this body, of course."

Polk looked down at the body. "He'll reveal himself, I have no doubt about that." He looked back up at Grave. "So, heard anything from Captain Morgan?"

"He cut his finger, I know that."

"Damned shame his being forced out. It's just not right. A man works his whole life at something and then is unceremoniously shown the door—by a damned machine no less."

Grave knew of Polk's dislike for simdroids, particularly the mayor, but decided not to chime in. "Yes, a shame."

Polk grew silent for a moment. He seemed to be struggling with what to say next. Finally, he decided. "You know, Grave, it's not my place to give advice, but if I were in your shoes, I'd bring Morgan up to speed on the case. He's not the smartest crab in the ocean, of course, but he has stumbled on a solution more times than not."

Grave was happy to have the advice. "That's a good idea. Thanks, Jeremy."

Polk sighed. "Well, then, till the morrow, good sir, at the morgue."

"Aren't you coming to the stadium?"

"No, it's past my bedtime, and besides, I'm just a poor old medical examiner, not a damned sleuth."

Grave chuckled. "All right, till tomorrow. I'll give June a call so we can begin first thing."

Polk nodded and walked away, leaving Grave standing next to the body, which was being carefully transferred to a stretcher by Polk's team. "Okay, Phil, I guess you've got this."

Phil nodded. "Right, sir."

Grave looked back at Gnote's house, where Loblolly and God were standing, waiting for instructions. He wasn't too keen on God's decision to become Alex Cross. In fact, he was warming to the idea of having God on his team.

He walked toward the house. They had work to do and people waiting at the stadium. With any luck, the Surround Vision replay would lead them to the killer or killers—and maybe even more bodies.

He waved at his detectives and God waved back.

36

Ramrod Stadium, home of the perennially winless Crab Cove Red Claws, was lit up like, well, a stadium lit up at night. Without a crowd, everything looked outrageously garish, from the bright red seats in the lower sections to the blinding yellow seats up top. Grave had watched a game from up there once, or at least part of one. The seats were so high he could barely make out what the players were doing on the field, which at that altitude looked like a green postage stamp with white lines.

He spotted June first. She was seated at a console in the center of the field, along with a simdroid technician who was obviously there to walk them through the Surround Vision replay. As he walked toward her from the end zone, he spotted the others—Charlize, Smithers, Loblolly, and God—sitting on the home team bench. He motioned them to join him at the console.

"Come on, guys, over here." He turned to June. "Hey, June, how's Rippley?"

June frowned. "Depressed, really depressed. But thanks for freeing up Barry. He's doing his best to cheer her up."

Grave nodded. "It's a mess, isn't it?"

"More than that, what with this unknown third victim."

"Right, right, so are you guys going to be able to make it tomorrow morning? I'll send a police cruiser for you, if you want."

"No, I'd rather drive. It calms me."

"I know what you mean."

She laughed. "But I don't know how you do it with that gospel music. When you arrived, the music echoed through the stadium for at least twenty seconds."

Grave shrugged. "I know, I know." He looked at the technician. "So, are we ready to do this?"

"Yes," said June. "Ricky here will take us through it."

"Okay." He turned and greeted the others. "Everyone here?"

"Except my Pine Cone," said Loblolly. "She's still out there, over the bay somewhere, trying to keep pace with that boat."

Grave nodded. "I'm sure she'll be okay. Any word from the Coast Guard?"

"Nothing yet."

He pointed at Ricky. "Ricky, how do we do this?"

Ricky, a generic male simdroid who looked like no man and every man, pointed at his console. "I control everything from here. The replay is timestamped, so give me a time and I'll take you right to it. And like most recordings, we can go forward, back, stop, and so on. When we turn off the stadium lights, you'll see a faithful one-to-one look at the town square, as it was at that particular time." He stopped and looked at each of them. "Any questions?"

God stepped forward. "I've never actually been in one of these Surround Vision things. Is it like a hologram?"

Ricky smiled. It was a silly question, but he decided to indulge God. "I get that question all the time. No, not really. It's about three generations forward from holograms. You'll be able to see everything in three dimensions, of course, but the clarity is much better than a hologram. If need be, we can zoom in and find the ants crawling in the grass. In short, if there are clues to be found in the town square, Surround Vision will help you find them." Ricky took God's nod as a signal of understanding and turned back to Grave. "Where would you like to begin?"

Grave knew exactly where. "Friday evening at eight o'clock."

Ricky punched a few buttons. The stadium lights went out and they were all suddenly standing in the center of the gazebo on town square.

It was night, and people in and around the square were frozen in the positions they occupied at exactly eight o'clock that night. There were a lot of tourists in *I Survived Crab Cove* sweatshirts, some looking happy but most looking tired from a full day trying to do everything there was to do in Crab Cove. In all, there must have been a hundred or more people in and around the town square.

"Amazing," said Grave. "All right, everybody. Let's head on over to Skunk 'n Donuts. I want to check out the argument between Ann and Grace, which should be starting right about now." He turned to Ricky. "How do I signal you from way over there?"

Ricky handed him a small controller. "I've switched control to you. Just push the buttons. It's exactly like your home version of Surround Vision. If you run into trouble, I'll be here in the gazebo."

"Great," said Grave. "Come on, folks, let's go."

They walked across the square and Main Street and went up to the window of the donut shop. He could see Grace and Ann through the window. Grace was looking up at Ann, who appeared to be just slipping into the booth, carrying a blue canvas shopping bag from Vac-o-Mac.

"Looks like we timed this just right," said Grave. "Ann is just arriving." He motioned to Smithers. "Get closer, Smithers. We need your lip-reading skills now."

Smithers-Watson pressed his nose against the glass. "Okay, whenever you're ready, sir."

"Right, here we go."

He pressed PLAY and Ann and Grace sprang to life, Smithers doing his best to translate their moving lips into words as quickly as he could.

GRACE: Well, it's about time.
ANN: Sorry, that damned boss of mine.
GRACE: Do you want anything? Coffee? Donut?
ANN: No, what I want is to call this off.
GRACE: Not a chance. We have to do this. It's the only way.
ANN: Keep your voice down. And it's not the only way.
GRACE: Screw my voice. We have to do this. You know that.
ANN: What if it goes sideways? I mean, there's a killer out there.
GRACE: We've gone through this over and over. The plan will work.

ANN: *I'm not so sure anymore. It seems too risky.*
GRACE: *We can't live our lives in fear, Ann.*
ANN: *I don't know.*
GRACE: *Listen, in ten minutes it will all be over. Think of it. Freedom. A new freakin' life.*
ANN: *I guess you're right. Okay, let's do this.*
GRACE: *Great, let's hit the bathroom first.*

The two of them stood up and disappeared into the women's bathroom.

"That's it, sir," said Smithers.

"Okay," said Grave, hitting the PAUSE button. "What did we learn?"

"They have a plan," said Charlize, "and they know the killer is out there."

"And they know that killing is on the agenda," said Loblolly.

"But the plan, whatever it was, will go wrong," said God.

"Yes," said Grave. "Let's watch it unfold."

Grave turned back to the window and hit PLAY, then FAST FORWARD until Ann and Grace reappeared from the bathroom. Then he hit PAUSE again. "Okay, here they come." He turned to Charlize. "If they split up, you and Smithers stay on Ann. If you want me to pause for any reason, just shout out."

"Okay."

"The rest of you, stay with me."

Everyone nodded, and Grave hit PLAY. The two women walked through the shop and out the front door. Ann immediately turned left, with Charlize and Smithers on her heels. Grace took two steps toward the square and slowly faded to invisibility.

Grave hit PAUSE. "Okay, she's heading to her death. Let's move to the spot in the grass where we found her body."

They walked across Main Street and down a path past the gazebo, where two men were playing chess. "I want to talk to those guys again," said Grave.

"I think Charlize and Smithers have already talked with them," said Loblolly.

"And I have, too," said God.

"Okay, we'll compare notes at some point and decide how to proceed with them."

He suddenly stopped. "Here's the spot where we found the body. Let's see how this plays out."

He hit PLAY and waited for the murder to happen. For a few seconds, nothing happened. A few seconds later, nothing continued to happen. He hit PAUSE. "We should have seen something by now."

"No," said June. "The thing about invisibility is that you have to move slowly. If you move too quickly, you create a ripple in the air, which can be seen. Remember, that's why we named Rippley, Rippley."

Grave nodded. "Okay, then." He hit PLAY again and waited. Suddenly a ripple arced across the square as if something was diving down toward them. He hit pause. "What in the world is that?"

June threw up her hands. "I don't know, but whatever that is appears to be flying."

Grave hit PLAY and the diving ripple stopped six feet off the ground. Other ripples began flailing at the rippling object. They looked like arms.

Grave hit PAUSE. "Whatever that first ripple was, Grace appears to be flailing her arms at it."

"It's a ploy," said God. "To make her visible to the killer."

"Who should be coming next," said Loblolly.

Grave nodded and hit PLAY again. A third ripple suddenly appeared with what looked like arms reaching out for Grace. Seconds later, the ripple that was Grace Gnote fell to the ground and disappeared.

Grave and the others watched as a ripple rose in the air and flew away.

Grave hit PAUSE. "I saw wings. That was a bird."

Charlize and Smithers came running up.

"Not just a bird," said Charlize. "That was a seagull."

"An invisible seagull," said Grave.

"And I know just which one," said Charlize.

Grave raised a brow. "You're not thinking of Horace, are you?"

"No, sir. Remember the McLachlan case? There were two birds, both implanted with neural nodes. Horace was one, and the other was named Arnold. And Arnold was stolen by Chester Clink."

Grave blinked at *Clink*. "But snapping necks isn't his M.O."

Charlize nodded. "It's curious, I admit that, but on the other hand, Ann's murder might fit."

"Well, the stab wounds, maybe, but he isn't one to just drop a body. He's all about presentation."

"Sir, if I may," said God. "I'll be updating my software to become a forensic psychologist, just like Alex Cross. I can give you my analysis in the morning."

Grave chuckled. "That will be helpful, God." He turned to the others. "Okay, let's rerun this and see if we pick up anything else."

He lifted the controller and hit REWIND.

37

The seagull dived, Grace threw up her rippling hands, and then the killer jumped in and snapped her neck. Again and again they played the tape but it wasn't until the fourth replay that Smithers nearly jumped out of his simskin. "Over there, another ripple."

They moved to a spot close to the chess players, who had seemed oblivious to everything going on around them during the murder of Grace Gnote.

Grave rewound the tape, then hit PLAY. They watched as a ripple suddenly appeared behind one of the chess payers. It looked like a small person who had startled and then run away at great speed. "Another invisible person, but who?"

"Can't be the body we found on the beach," said Loblolly. "This one's too small, maybe a young boy or girl."

Grave was puzzled. "Why would a child be here at this hour? And hovering by the chess players? What's up with that?"

"There's something not quite right about them," said Charlize. "They may be doing more than just playing chess."

"Like what?"

"Dunno, but perhaps Rippley can shed some light on this."

Grave nodded. "I'll see her in the morning, at the morgue. The good news is, the child is a witness, and may know more than we're seeing here on the replays."

"Right," said Charlize. "But she might also be a future victim, assuming the killer saw her run away."

Grave turned to June. "If you can find out anything tonight, that would be great. At any rate, talk to her and give me a call as soon as you know anything."

"No problem," said June. "I'll try to get back to you this evening."

Grave nodded. "Good." He turned to the others. "Okay, then," said Grave. "Let's move on to Ann. I'll rewind the tape to eight thirty and then we can move to Vac-o-Mac and see what she does."

The walk to the Vac-o-Mac took only a minute. They could see Ann through the window, having what appeared to be a heated argument with her boss. Finally, she threw some sales tickets in the air and stormed out of the store, almost instantly becoming invisible.

The team looked this way and that, but Ann was just gone.

"She's moving slowly," said Smithers. "To avoid detection."

"Yes," said Grave. "No ripples, at least not yet."

"Sir," said God. "Won't she be moving to the parking lot?"

"Yes, of course, and the shortest path is the sidewalk along Blue Crab Boulevard. Come on."

He walked away from the store and crossed Main Street to reach the sidewalk along Blue Crab Boulevard, everyone else trailing behind him. They saw nothing along the way, and when they reached the parking lot, they could see a car pulling out and speeding away.

Grave shook his head. "Stupid of me. We should rewind the tape and wait for her here."

He pressed REWIND, then STOP, then PLAY. "Okay, let's get to the car and watch what happens. Look for any ripples."

They surrounded the car and waited. After a few minutes, the passenger door opened and then closed.

Grave hit PAUSE. "She's in the car."

"It must be a driverless car," said Loblolly. "She got in on the wrong side."

"Okay, let's see what happens," said Grave. He pressed PLAY and they all watched as a ripple suddenly erupted inside the car. It lasted only an instant, and then the hovercruiser moved away, picking up speed as it sped southbound on Imperial Avenue.

"What was that?" said Charlize.
"Looked like a tussle," said Loblolly.
"More like a punch," said Smithers-Watson."
"God only knows," said God.

59

38

Grave's mind reeled as he pondered the case to the sound of gospel music. Two dead women. One dead man, identity unknown, possibly Cliff Gnote. One invisible seagull. Two chess players. One invisible child, identity unknown. Two missing cars. Three missing drones. One murderer? Two? And Chester Clink as a possible cherry on top?

How could he possibly brief the mayor at noon tomorrow? He'd be thrown out on his ear. On the other hand, he'd been in this situation before, when the solution to a seemingly unsolvable crime suddenly clicks into place, every detail aligning, every box checked.

He pulled into the parking lot and turned off the ignition.

"Well, that was quite a sigh," said Barry.

"Yes, this damned case. I don't suppose you have any insights on what we just watched."

"Not really. I zoomed around the square several times while you were watching the murders unfold, but I didn't see anything unusual. Just town square on Friday and Saturday night."

"And Saturday night was a complete bust. No ripples at all."

"Of course the chess players were there again right after the concert. That seemed a little odd to me."

"Yes, but no little-child ripples. God, do you think she's dead, too?"

"Maybe, possibly. Of course, do we know for sure that we're dealing with an invisible child? Perhaps it was a midget or a dwarf. And if so, maybe he or she is a murderer or an accomplice. Maybe the one who killed the man on the beach and fled on the boat."

Grave rolled his eyes. "Oh, I'm sure the mayor will be thrilled with that theory."

"Sorry, just thinking out loud."

Grave shook his head. "How in the world am I going to brief the mayor?"

"Perhaps we can sort this all out at tomorrow's meeting. I mean, God will be Alex Cross, right, forensic psychologist extraordinaire?"

Grave couldn't help chuckling. "We can only hope."

Barry lifted into the air. "Come on, let's get inside. I'm sure a glass of Duct Tape Chardonnay will set you right—or at least make you sleepy."

Grave extricated himself from the little car and followed Barry to the lighthouse he now called home. He pushed open the door and almost stepped on his scientist guest, Red, the simcrab carcinologist, who skittered sideways just in time to avoid Grave's foot.

"Hey," said Red. "Watch what you're doing."

"Sorry," said Grave. "How are you, Red?"

The little simcrab sighed. "Not so good. Or rather, I'm fine but the crabs in the bay are in a steep decline. I've just been going over the data. If we can't turn this around, you can say goodbye to crabs—and Crab Cove for that matter—in about ten years."

Grave nodded. You only had to look at the astronomical price of crabs these days to know that something bad was happening. "I'm sorry to hear that. Say, would you like to join me for a late dinner?"

"I don't eat. You know that."

"Well, we could talk."

Red considered it, then waved a claw. "No, I don't think so. I need to go over the data. Maybe I'm missing something."

Missing something, thought Grave. *I'm certainly missing something. Maybe a lot of somethings.* "All right, if you need anything, give Roderick a ring."

"I can't think of what I'd need from him, but okay, thanks."

Red skittered across the room, sat down at the smallest laptop Grave had ever seen, and began clacking away at the keyboard.

Grave turned and started walking up the spiral staircase. As he climbed he could hear the sound of *Casablanca* playing in the kitchen. Roderick would no doubt be sitting near the piano, watching Sam play.

39

Rippley looked down at the body she had just made visible and then quickly jumped down from Polk's stool. "It's him, Cliff Gnote. I guess I was wrong about him. I thought he killed Grace. He certainly threatened to more than once outside the school."

Gave blinked. "He came to your house?"

"Yes, lurked about, tried to talk to Grace. We always chased him away."

Grave turned to June. "You chased this big guy away?"

"No, not me. We got one of our students, Wayne Dough, to do the chasing."

You mean Chester Clink, thought Grave. "And how did that go?"

"Well, they almost came to blows the first time, but by the third time, Wayne took him aside and gave him a good talking to. We never saw him after that."

"Until now," said Rippley.

"Okay, thanks." Grave turned to Polk. "Any idea about cause of death and time of death?"

Polk pulled the sheet down farther on the body. "I think that's pretty clear. Have a look."

Grave bent over the body. The knife work was unmistakable. "Chester Clink."

June gasped. "The serial killer?"

"Yes."

"Wait, I thought he only killed women?"

Grave nodded. "That's been the case so far—until now."

"I don't understand. Why would Chester Clink have anything to do with Cliff Gnote?"

Grave turned to Barry, who had been hovering in the corner. "Barry, please project the last known photograph of Chester Clink."

"Yes, sir, retrieving." He positioned himself in front of the far wall. After a few seconds of clicks and buzzes, the image of Chester Clink appeared on the wall.

June and Rippley squinted at the image, then shrugged.

"Wait," said Grave. "You don't recognize him?"

"Nope," said Rippley.

June shook her head, too. "If that's Clink, I'm sure I've never seen him before."

Grave didn't know quite what to say to that. "But the way you first described Wayne John Dough, I thought for sure it was Chester Clink."

Had Chester Clink had cosmetic surgery? Were they dealing with a copycat killer? He turned to Polk. "Are you sure it was Chester Clink?"

"If it wasn't, we have a copycat at the top of his game. I'd swear those wounds were made not just by Clink, but by the same damned knife. There's a little nick in Clink's blade, about two inches down from the point, and by god, these wounds show exactly that."

Grave nodded. "Maybe he's changed his appearance. It's easy to do these days."

Polk waggled his head. "Could be. There's a woman in my apartment building who changes her look with each birthday. It's kind of creepy, but whatever."

"Okay, then, what about time of death?"

"I'd say Sunday afternoon. Just shortly before the body was discovered."

Perhaps the person on the boat is our killer, Grave thought. He wondered if the Coast Guard had intercepted it and whether Loblolly's drone, Pine Cone, had reported in.

"Thanks, Jeremy. I think we're done here, but if anything else comes up, let me know."

"No problem."

Grave turned to June and Rippley. "But before you go, I have a few questions about one of your former students."

40

The drive from the morgue to Captain Morgan's new houseboat had only taken a few minutes, just enough time for Grave to review the case in his head and formulate questions for Captain Morgan.

The latest piece of information to click into place was the fact that a little girl named Penelope Goodlove had apparently been at the town square when Grace Gnote was killed. Rippley had explained that Penelope had often talked about the chess players in the square and that she was investigating them for treason. Perhaps she had seen the murder, perhaps not, but she was certainly the ripple they saw running from the square. At any rate, he had had his drone Barry give her a call to invite her to the station for questioning.

As for now, though, his first need was to talk with Captain Morgan, lay out the case, and get his advice on how best to proceed, particularly with the mayor's meeting and a news conference coming up later in the day.

Captain Morgan's new houseboat was far from new. In fact, it looked like it had just been refloated after years at the bottom of the cove. Morgan, alerted by the gospel music, came out on deck, a scowl on his face. He was shouting words, that was clear, but the words could not break through the force field of the music that surrounded the car. Grave turned off the ignition, and the music died away.

Morgan was still shouting. "I said, turn off that damned music." And then he realized the music had stopped and began shaking his head. "What do you want, Grave?"

Grave got out of the car. "Permission to come aboard, Captain."

Morgan rolled his eyes and beckoned him to board. "What is it now, Grave? I'm very busy, you know. In fact, I'm so busy, I can't imagine how I ever had time for work."

Grave looked at Morgan's left hand. The tips of three fingers were heavily bandaged. "So, how's the wood carving going?"

Morgan looked at his hand. "Very funny."

"A man needs a hobby."

"Yeah, right. Anyway, come on in. Amanda's here, and I think you'll be interested in what she has to say."

Grave blinked. "Snoot? What's she doing here?"

Morgan flapped his arms. Every question now seemed to annoy him. "Come on, I'll let her explain. Some crazy shit is going down."

41

Detective Charlize Holmes puffed at her tobaccoless simpipe and paced back and forth in the squad room as Dr. Smithers-Watson watched in silence. He knew better than to interrupt her when she was processing data, even though he was ready to burst with his own conclusions about their time in the town square, particularly their conversation with the two chess players.

He checked his watch. Grave was overdue for the morning meeting. Not surprising, but still annoying. He looked back at Charlize, who was still pacing. Frustrated, he turned his attention elsewhere. He could see Loblolly sitting alone at her desk, looking very glum. Her personal drone had apparently gone missing or worse. He thought briefly about leaving Charlize to her musings and going over to Loblolly to offer some moral support.

But before he could do anything, Retective Tilda Must had come out of nowhere and pulled up a chair next to him. Must, a simdroid who resembled the young Tilda Swinton, was a big fan of Charlize's. Her official job was to review recently closed cases and point out places where the investigation or a detective's actions could have been improved, resulting in a swifter arrest and a stronger case for prosecutors. She loved Charlize, who rarely made mistakes, and when she did, they were always well-reasoned and logical, unlike Grave.

She leaned in and whispered to Smithers-Watson. "Don't you just love the way she paces when she's processing?"

Smithers-Watson shrugged. "I guess."

"Oh, I find it absolutely exhilarating. So, are we close to solving these murders?"

Smithers-Watson nodded. "I have no doubt we shall have a solution forthwith, as well as a solution to a new crime as yet unaddressed."

"New? What new case?"

Smithers-Watson held up a hand. "Too early to discuss, but you'll learn about it soon enough."

Must gave him a sly smile. "Oh, I'm sure I will. Speaking of which, I want you to know how much I admire the work that you and Charlize do for us each day."

"Us?"

"You know, the entire force. And let me tell you, when the changes that need to be made are made, the two of you will be at the top of the detectives list."

Smithers-Watson frowned. "What are you talking about?"

Again the sly smile. "Morgan is out and a new captain will come in. I have no doubt she'll elevate the two of you on the first day."

He blinked at *she*. "What are you saying?"

"Nothing, at least not yet. You'll find out soon enough."

"Find out what?"

"Let's just say I have the ear of the mayor."

He rolled his eyes. "Why are you speaking in riddles?"

42

Detective Polly Loblolly was in a funk. A complete funk. She had just taken a call from the Coast Guard, informing her that the fleeing boat had been overtaken, but upon boarding, they had found nothing and no one. The boat had been abandoned five miles off the Atlantic coast. The controls were set on autopilot, so there was every possibility that the boat had been empty when it left the docks. A misdirection perhaps, which would have allowed the murderer to escape, possibly in one of the missing hovercruisers.

But the worst news was that there was no sign of her drone, Pine Cone, who had apparently been lost at sea. Every attempt at contact had failed, at least so far. Pine Cone was resourceful and not prone to give up, so Loblolly held on to the hope that the drone would somehow miraculously appear or at least make contact.

Her funk was interrupted as someone nearby cleared their throat. Loblolly looked up. *Oh, my god, it's Tilda Must. And what the hell does that smile mean? Jesus, I've never seen her smile.* "Morning, retective."

"Good morning, detective. Sorry to interrupt you. I see you're deep in thought."

Loblolly nodded, trying hard not break down in tears. "Yes, just got some bad news."

"Oh?"

"We were chasing a suspect fleeing on a boat, but as it turns out, the boat was empty, cruising on autopilot."

"A ruse."

"Yes, possibly."

Must gave her that same sly smile. "So, anyway, I just wanted to know that you've made a big, positive impact on this police force, and that will be remembered when the time comes."

Loblolly frowned. "What time is that?"

The smile deepened. "Why, when a new captain comes on board."

Loblolly sighed. A new captain was the least of her concerns. "Whatever."

"No, no, big changes are coming for you. In fact, I can guarantee it."

Loblolly gave her an appraising look. "What does *that* mean?"

Must stood and looked down at her. "Well, it's too soon to say, but mark my words, good things are coming for you."

And with that, she turned and walked away, heading for the desk of Detective Barry Blunt. Loblolly shrugged and then let out a big sigh. "Where in the hell are you, Pine Cone?"

43

Grave's sighs were obliterated by the gospel music playing for the entire town to hear. He had a lot of sigh-inducing things to think about, so he drove more slowly than usual. There was just so much to sort out, and Captain Morgan had been as confused as he was now. Everything pointed to Chester Clink. Then again, a lot of things pointed away from Chester Clink. Perhaps the only worthwhile action item was his decision at the morgue to bring in Wayne John Dough for questioning. Then they could decide whether the man was a copycat killer, an innocent bystander, or a surgically altered Chester Clink himself.

Dough's name alone was reason for suspicion. Wayne was a common name for serial killers: John Wayne Gacy, Elmer Wayne Henley, Monty Wayne Lamb, Alexander Wayne Watson, Jr., and Wayne Williams were legendary serial killers. Also, John Dough had to be a play on John Doe. If Clink had to make up a name for himself, Wayne John Dough would have certainly given him a laugh.

Morgan thought there was more than one killer involved, and perhaps he was right. It was unlike Clink to simply snap a person's neck. Unless, of course, he wanted to get Grace out of the way so he could attack Ann. Grave thought back to the Surround Vision replay and shook his head. Whoever abducted and killed Ann didn't have to kill Grace. Yes, the two women had been walking to the parking lot, but at different times and from different directions.

Grave hoped that Dr. Alex Cross, one-time God, would be able to help out, give them all a psychological profile of the killer or killers when they met this morning to discuss the case.

Grave sighed again. The gospel singers swallowed it up.

Then there was the matter of the mayor and what Snoot had learned. He rolled his eyes. They just couldn't let that stand.

Not now, not ever.

44

Sergeant Barry Blunt had never felt so alone and out of touch in his life. Everyone else was busy at their desks, going over their notes in preparation for this morning's meeting. Charlize and Smithers were in an animated conversation in one corner, and Loblolly was sitting silently at her desk. He knew she was worried about her drone, Pine Cone, who had not yet returned from the pursuit of what appeared to be a getaway boat. Officer Larry, aka God, was also missing, whereabouts unknown.

That left Blunt sitting alone at his desk with little more to do than shuffle paper and deal with the occasional petty crime. And now things were about to get a lot worse. Retective Tilda Must was walking his way, a sly smile on her face.

Blunt didn't have a problem with her—she usually reserved her scorn for Grave—but since he had never seen her smile, he was apprehensive about what was about to happen. He considered suddenly rising from his desk and racing for the bathroom, but that thought went flying when she slipped into the chair opposite him.

"How are you today, Sergeant Blunt?" She was still smiling in that funny way. She knew something he didn't and was about to burst with the news. Of what, he had no idea.

"Um—"

She burst. "Let me get straight to the point. I know you and that Detective Grave person hate me, but that will soon be water under the bridge, crabs in the pot, I assure you."

Blunt wasn't sure what to say first. Should he deny Grave's hatred when everyone knew it was true? Or should he focus on the bridge, the water, the crab, and the pot?

In his blank-faced confusion, she pressed on. "There will be changes, of course. Many changes, but all meant to make things better around here, I assure you."

Blunt finally found his voice. "What are you talking about?"

She gave him that grin again, one that suggested the eating of human waste or the consumption of a canary by a guilty cat. She slapped her hand down on his desk. "I have applied for the captaincy."

Blunt's mouth dropped open. "You've *what?*"

"Applied. For Morgan's job." She began to giggle or at least attempted a giggle. It came out more like a shrill hiccup. "Isn't that great?"

Blunt tried to recover. "Well, that *is* news. Then again, I'm sure a lot of people have applied, and there will be a host of external candidates."

Must scoffed. "They don't stand a chance against me. Besides, the mayor thinks I'm a lock for the position."

Blunt's eyes went wide. "What? He really said that?"

"Yes, isn't it wonderful? Now, what I'd like you to do is consider what changes you'd like to see in the department. I assure you, I will have an open-door policy right from the start."

"Um, I'll definitely give that some thought."

"Excellent," she said, standing. "I'm glad we had this little talk."

She didn't give him a chance to reply. She just turned and walked away, searching for the next "future employee" to talk to.

"Oh, my god," said Barry to himself. "Wait till Grave finds out about this."

He thought to send a message to Grave immediately, but a young red-headed girl entering the station caught his attention. She couldn't have been more than eight or nine years old, but she walked into the station with a confidence and demeanor suggesting that she was more like nine going on thirty. She was about four feet tall, a little short for her age, and thin, with green eyes that sparkled with youth and enthusiasm. Freckles defined her face and neck, and she seemed to have some sort of mark on her face. She was wearing a school uniform. White blouse, red and white striped vest, a matching skirt that rested just above her knees, revealing two inches of freckled flesh between the skirt and her white knee sox. Blunt tried to think of the school's name, but the name escaped him. He also had the feeling that he had seen her before.

The girl scanned the squad room and settled on Blunt as her target, giving him a quick nod and walking straight for him. From the look on her face, she had serious business to discuss.

Blunt gave her a quick smile as she came up to his desk and hovered over him. "What can I do for you, young lady?"

"Sergeant, my name is Penelope Goodlove." She handed him a business card that read *Penelope Goodlove, Principal Investigator, The Penelope Goodlove Invisible Detective Agency.*

Her voice was deeper than expected, and her breath smelled of peppermint. *Goodlove, Goodlove, he thought. Where have I heard that name?* He reached out his hand. "Sergeant Barry Blunt. Happy to meet you, um, detective."

She ignored his hand. "Let me get right to the point, Sergeant. I have reason to believe that a crime of the highest order has been committed, and I am here to report it."

Blunt smiled. She was so cute. He could see now that the mark on her face was a birthmark in the shape of an owl. "A crime, you say?" He looked at the owl again, perhaps a second too long.

"Yes, and why are you smiling?" She immediately put her hand over her cheek.

Blunt tried to recover. "Oh, no, it's not that. No, not at all. I was thinking how *wonderful* it is to have a citizen report a crime. I mean, a *principal investigator.*"

She gave him a skeptical look and dropped her hand to her side. "Anyway, you need to immediately arrest two people."

"And who might they be?"

She pulled out a little electronic notebook. "First, we have one Lev Korsokov, a manager at the Crab Cove Tourist Bureau."

She turned the notebook around so Blunt could see a photo of the man.

"Uh-huh," said Blunt. "And two?"

"Two, we have one Dewey Ditts, a ground crew member at the Mars Terminal."

She showed him a pic.

"And what sort of crime have they committed?"

She took a deep breath. "They play chess in the town square."

"That's not a crime."

She frowned at him. "They play chess *while committing a crime*."

"And that crime would be?"

"Espionage, treason. They are only pretending to play chess. What they are really doing is exchanging information."

"And you've overheard them somehow, um, plotting?"

"Yes, I mean no. I mean I can make myself invisible."

Blunt leaned forward. "Oh, oh, I thought I recognized you. You go to Rippley's school, right?"

She beamed. "Actually, I've graduated."

"Good, good. Okay, then. You observed the two chess players exchanging information."

"Exactly, but not through the spoken word. They're exchanging information by means of memory straws inserted into the black king and the white king. Each wins every other game, you see, so the wins are a form of communication."

Blunt remained skeptical. "Memory straws?"

"Yes, inserted into chess pieces. I've seen them pocket the kings after each game. So now you need to arrest them."

Blunt shook his head. "We can't just go arrest people for playing chess."

"But the security of our nation is at risk, and the Mars Colony as well."

Blunt puffed out his cheeks. "Okay, here's what I can do. If what you say is true, they're committing a federal crime. If you'll have a seat, I'll give our contact at the FBI a call. Then you can give him the information. Does that work for you?"

As she nodded, the doors to the station slammed open and Grave walked in, Barry hovering by his shoulder. Grave spotted her from across the room. "Penelope Goodlove, you're just the little girl I need to talk to."

45

Everyone but Blunt, who was forbidden, and God, who was late, moved to the conference room to interview little Penelope Goodlove, who was mystified by the new level of attention she was receiving.

"What's this all about?" she said "I'm just here to report a crime."

"So I hear, Penny," said Grave, "but we have some questions regarding your whereabouts on Friday evening."

Penelope frowned. "First of all, don't call me Penny. The name is Penelope." She waited until everyone nodded. "Second, I was in the town square, collecting information that I hope will lead to the immediate arrest of two men who play chess but don't know how to play chess."

Smithers-Watson spoke up. "I knew it." He turned to Charlize. "I told you I saw him move the bishop forward rather than diagonally."

"That would be Ditts," said Penelope. "He does that all the time."

"And the other gentleman moves his knights the same way he moves his pawns," said Smithers-Watson.

"That would be Korsokov," said Penelope. "He can't play at all."

Grave raised his voice. "That's all very interesting, but that's not why we're here. Save all that for the FBI." He looked at his watch. "In the meantime, let's stick with Friday night, shall we?"

Penelope nodded. "Okay, what do you want to know?"

"We know about the chess players. What else did you see?"

Her lips began to quiver. "I'm not sure. Something bad I think."

"Ripples, right? Made by invisible people."

She nodded.

"And you were invisible, too."

"Yes, that was the only way I could get close to Ditts and Korsokov. There's nothing wrong with that, is there?"

Grave shook his head. "No, the law hasn't caught up with invisibility yet."

She nodded. "It looked like someone was being attacked. It scared me and I ran."

"Right, the CCTV cameras caught your ripples as you fled."

Penelope gave him a questioning look. "If you already know that, why am I here?"

"Good question. We'd like to learn more about your time in town square. Did you go there every day?"

"Most days, for the past month or so. They usually play chess late in the day, just before dark, but sometimes they play—or at least pretend to play—well into the night."

"On those other days, did you ever see any ripples? You know, other invisible people on the square?"

She shook her head. "No, only that one night, Friday."

"And on that night, how many different ripples did you see?"

She looked at the ceiling. "Um, three. No, four."

"Four?"

"Yes, there were ripples that looked like flailing arms, there were ripples that looked like a man running, there were ripples that looked like wings—imagine that, an invisible bird—and there were ripples that looked like a shorter man running by me as I fled the square."

Grave looked around the room. "Really? We must have missed that last one."

Penelope smiled. "I'm glad I could help."

"Tell me, Penelope, did you recognize any of the people causing the ripples?"

"No, but Rippley has already told me about Grace and Ann. And I don't know who the men were." She smiled. "Or that bird."

Grave sat back in his chair. "Does anyone else have questions?"

Charlize pushed back her chair and began pacing back and forth along the length of the table, keeping her eyes fixed on Penelope. "Thank you for that additional piece of information—the running man. But so far we've only talked about one sense, sight. Now I'd like to ask you about your other senses. As all these ripples happened around you, did you smell anything or hear anything?"

Penelope pursed her lips. "Um, the only thing I smelled was that rotten-egg smell that clings to anyone who's been around the fuel they use for those new plasma-drive launch vehicles. Ditts wreaked of it."

Charlize nodded. "Okay, and what about hearing. When all this went down, did Grace or her attacker make any sounds?"

Penelope brightened. "Yes, I'd completely forgotten about it, but yes, I did hear something."

"And . . ."

"Someone shouted 'no' just before it all happened."

"No?"

"Yes, that's what made me turn in their direction."

"So, Grace saw her attacker and shouted 'no,' is that what you're saying?"

Penelope shook her head. "No, it was a man's voice."

"Not Grace?"

"No, it sounded like a warning, like he wanted to stop what was about to happen."

Charlize stopped pacing. "A man attacks a woman but warns her first."

Penelope sighed heavily. "I know this is going to sound crazy, but I had the distinct feeling that the voice was coming from the bird. I know, I know, a talking bird. Ridiculous, but that's what I sensed."

Charlize looked at Grave, raised an eyebrow, and then turned back to Penelope. "Ridiculous or not, such birds do exist."

Penelope giggled. "How odd—and *wonderful*."

Charlize bowed toward Penelope. "Thank you for your help." She turned to Grave. "I have no further questions." She returned to her chair and sat down, whispering to Smithers-Watson, who nodded his head vigorously.

Grave looked around the room. "Anyone else?"

Loblolly raised her hand. "Just a couple of questions, about the relationships in your particular class. As I understand it, you were in the same class as Grace, Ann, and two others."

"Um, actually three, but Jack Friendly left the class early for another remedial class. He just didn't get it. Otherwise, there was Malcolm Spitzer and Wayne John Dough."

"And how did you all get along?"

"What do you mean?"

"I mean were you friendly? Did some of you get along better than others of you?"

"Oh, I see what you mean. Well, Grace and Ann bonded almost immediately, I'm not sure why."

"How did you get along with them?"

She smiled. "Pretty good. No, really good. You know, it was like I was their little sister. That kind of thing."

"What about this Spitzer person."

Penelope rolled her eyes and giggled. "He was so shy. I think he liked all of us, but he just couldn't bring himself to interact with us other than quick smiles."

"I see. Now, what about Wayne John Dough?"

Penelope frowned. "I didn't like him."

"Oh?"

"No, there was something off about him. The looks he gave me and the others were kind of creepy."

"Creepy? How?"

Penelope shuddered. "Like he was looking through you, appraising you, looking for weaknesses."

"And how did he get along with Grace and Ann?"

"Not at all. They basically shunned him. I think they sensed what I sensed, that he was bad news."

Loblolly bit her lower lip, thinking about what to ask next. "Um, were there any specific incidents that might suggest animosity between them?"

Penelope shook her head. "No, it was just an overwhelming feeling of discomfort, for all of us. He would follow you with his eyes, those dark, dark, eyes." She shuddered again. "Creepy."

Loblolly nodded to Grave. "That's all I have, sir." She turned back to Penelope. "Thank you."

"You're welcome."

Grave looked around the room. "Anyone else?"

Everyone shook their heads.

"All right, then. Penelope, let me walk you back out to Sergeant Blunt's desk." He turned to the others. "Sit tight, we have a lot to discuss."

46

The last person Grave expected to see when he left the conference room with Penelope was FBI Agent Cliff "Bull" Montgomery. The two of them had butted heads over the years, but as the years went by and their relationship matured, they continued to butt heads, only with less face-to-face spittle.

"What the hell are you doing here?" said Grave by way of friendly greeting.

Bull barked back at him. "I was *invited*." He pointed at Sergeant Blunt. "By your *cloudy partner* here."

Penelope tugged at Grave's sleeve. "He's here to see me, about the chess players."

Bull nodded. "That's right, Grave, so let me take her off your hands."

Grave sneered at him. "Fine, you can use the small conference room. The big conference room is taken. Getting ready for a big meeting with the mayor."

"Ha! As if."

"No, really, I'm meeting the mayor at noon to discuss our news conference about the murders."

"Murders, shmurders, that's just not going to happen."

"And why not?"

"Because obviously you're not up to speed on the latest happenings in this town."

"Stop talking in riddles."

Bull chuckled. "Seems the mayor was just arrested for malfeasance in office, along with money laundering, bribery, and related charges." He looked down at Penelope. "And with the help of this little girl here, perhaps espionage and treason."

Shocked and delighted was not a word combination that Grave used often, but it seemed entirely appropriate in the moment. His face struggled to keep up with the mixed messages being sent by his brain, so he alternated between drop-jawed amazement and an insane giggle that startled Bull.

"Are you okay?"

Grave tried his best to regain his composure, but his brain began to lose control of the situation, pushing him further and further toward demented cackling. "Yes, yes, I'm fine. Are you sure about this?" He suppressed a cackle.

"Absolutely. You remember Agent Walters, right? He's the one who made the arrest. Oh, and you can probably forget about that news conference. The press is all over this. You've been bumped from the news cycle, my friend."

Grave felt suddenly at ease, as if his brain had opened a valve to release a near-explosive pressure. "Well, that is news. Good news, in fact. The mayor was pressuring us to solve the damned cases today."

Bull snorted. "People at the top have no patience, you know that."

"Exactly."

They seemed to have agreed on something for the first time and neither knew quite how to handle it.

"Well then," said Grave.

"Yes, so," said Bull.

"Right, right, well, um, the conference room is over there. If you need anything, Blunt can help you."

"Okay then," said Bull, turning to Penelope. "Shall we?"

"Indeed," said Penelope. "We have much to discuss."

As Grave watched them turn and walk into the small conference room, he caught sight of Retective Must sitting alone in the corner, glowering at him. There would be no Captain Must, and she knew it.

He gave her a quick smile and headed back into the conference room.

47

The news of Mayor Change's arrest sent a brief shock wave through the conference room, each person turning to the next with raised eyebrows, most silently mouthing the word *wow*.

"Okay," said Grave, rapping a knuckle on the table. "Plenty of time to discuss *that* news later. Let's get back to the case, shall we?"

Charlize raised a hand. "Sir, if I may."

"Yes?"

"I'd like to suggest that we discuss each victim first, rather than trying to sort out who the murderer or murderers are."

Grave nodded. "Okay, but first I think we should discuss Penelope Goodlove's testimony. What have we learned?"

Loblolly raised a hand. "Nothing much. She confirms everything we saw in the Surround Vision replay."

"But," said Smithers-Watson, "she added something that may be of immense importance to solving these cases."

"You mean the bird," said Grave.

"Yes, exactly," said Smithers-Watson. "For whatever reason, the bird was not there as part of the attack. It was trying to warn her."

Charlize jumped in. "Or warn the killer off."

Grave nodded. "Either way, it's puzzling. Perhaps Chester Clink murdered no one."

"But he is involved," said Charlize. "Somehow."

Grave looked around the room. "Anyone have anything else to say about Penelope's testimony?"

A lot of head shaking.

"Okay, then, let's turn back to Charlize's idea, and—" He suddenly stopped. "Anyone seen or heard from God, I mean whatshisname, Alex Cross?"

"Not a word," said Loblolly. "My guess is he's out shopping for his costume or maybe receiving his new forensic psychology programming."

Grave sighed. "All right, then, let's hope he arrives before we're finished. It would be nice to have the insights of a forensic psychologist." He pointed at Charlize. "Okay, proceed."

Charlize pushed back her chair and began pacing. "Let's take the victims, each in turn. Why would anyone want to kill them? Who are the likely suspects?"

She scanned the room, gauging their readiness to begin. All eyes were on her. "Let's start with Grace Gnote."

And they did.

48

God's absence continued as Grave and the others, save for Smoot and Blunt, discussed each of the three victims, their relationships, and any and all suspects. Charlize led the discussions with Smithers-Watson at the white board, writing down what was known and unknown. If Captain Morgan had been involved, he would have insisted on listing the known knowns, the unknown knowns, the known unknowns, and the unknown unknowns. Charlize always thought that was a useless exercise, so she boiled it all down to the knowns and unknowns. In the end, they had three columns, one each for Grace, Ann, and Cliff.

Under Grace's column, Smithers-Watson noted that Grace and Ann knew each other and also knew someone was out to at least do harm to Grace. They had a plan for dealing with it, but it wasn't clear what that plan was from their conversation at the Skunk 'n Donuts. Under suspects, he listed Cliff as prime, Wayne as secondary—from those creepy looks he had given both of the women—with Clink and Other as possibilities. Unresolved questions included why the invisible bird (presumably Clink's seagull, Arnold) had apparently tried to stop the killer or warn Grace.

The column for Ann was similar to Grace's except all the suspects— Cliff, Clink, Wayne, and Other—were given equal weight and an additional question was added, namely why had she taken invisibility training in the first place? They'd have the answer to that, of course, once the meeting concluded and they could get the student applications back from Blunt.

Cliff's column had more questions than facts. Who taught him the here and not of invisibility? Wayne seemed the logical choice, since they had talked, but could it have been another student or even a student of a student? And how did Clink fit in? According to Polk, the knife wounds were made by Clink's blade. As for suspects, Wayne, Clink, and Other held equal weight, at least at this point in the investigation.

After Charlize led them through the exercise, one thing was clear, at least to her. "We need to bring in Wayne for questioning. I think he might be the key to unraveling the entire puzzle."

Grave cleared his throat. "I agree. Barry tried to call him but his drone isn't picking up. We'll have to send someone to get him."

Loblolly raised her hand. "I'll go."

Grave shook his head. "I don't want you going alone." He looked at his watch. "Where in hell is God?"

Loblolly snorted. "I think you mean *in heaven*, sir."

As if on cue, God, or at least someone who used to be God, walked in. He was Dr. Alex Cross now, forensic psychologist extraordinaire, from his well-trimmed, grizzled beard, to his beige trench coat, to his blue shirt, to his maroon tie, to his dark gray suit. He had an air about him that suggested a calm confidence overlaid with a deep and abiding sadness.

He scanned the room as if he owned it, then nodded at Grave. "I see from the white board that you've started discussing suspects without me."

Grave shrugged. "We didn't know where you were."

"Understood."

Cross walked over to the white board and considered each column, alternately nodding and shaking his head. Finally, he took a deep breath and turned to face the team. "Let us begin."

49

Alex Cross waited until he had everyone's full attention, then began. "The killers are listed on this board behind me, but before I give you my take on exactly what happened and why, I think we need to review the types of serial killers out there and how our suspects might match up with one or more types."

"Sounds good," said Grave. "Go on."

"Okay," said Cross. "Now, as I go through these types, again, try to imagine how our suspects here might fit the bill."

Cross launched right in, identifying the four main types of serial killers as thrill seekers, mission-oriented, visionary killers, and power/control seekers.

Thrill seekers enjoy being pursued and outsmarting the police. They're fond of sending messages and keeping detailed records of their killings, including press clippings. They're organized but they don't necessarily plan things out in advance. They use weapons and it's typical that they rape the victim before killing them and hiding their body.

Cross paused. "We have weapons being used, but the victims weren't raped and were only hidden by their invisibility. Still, we may have to keep this one under consideration. The victims' invisibility may have disrupted their usual methods."

He then turned to mission-oriented serial killers, whom he described as killers who think they're helping society by ridding them of his victims: prostitutes, drug dealers, and so on. They're very organized. Each crime scene is nearly identical. Generally, they're easier to track down because they go after specific targets.

Cross stopped and looked around the room. "I don't think any of these killings are mission-based, so I think we can rule this one out. Now, on to the visionaries."

He described visionary serial killers as people who suffer from psychotic breaks. They sometimes think they're someone else or feel compelled to act because God, the Devil, or some unseen demon told them to. David Berkowitz, Son of Sam, is an example. He got his marching orders from a demon talking through a neighbor's dog. These killers are typically unorganized and easy to track down.

"I think we can rule out visionaries. The white board just doesn't support it. Now, on to the last type, the power seekers, the control freaks."

Cross explained that the power and control killers tend to have a history of childhood abuse, leaving them with feelings of inadequacy as adults. They're organized and enjoy terrorizing their victims. Screams and suffering excites them. They typically rape their victims, but it's never about sex. It's just another way to dominate their victims.

"I don't think we're dealing with the power seekers, at least not pure ones."

"Not pure ones?" said Grave. "What do you mean?"

"The crimes on the white board suggest a mix of the various types. Plus, there are other subcategories of serial killers."

"More than just the four types?"

"Exactly. There are *spree killers*, who kill one or more additional people after killing their selected victim. There are *lust killers*, killers who get off sexually by the act of killing. Then you have group killers, killers who form the equivalent of clubs, with killing a requirement for admission and continuing membership. And, of course, there are mass murderers, but that isn't what we're dealing with here."

Loblolly raised her hand. "You haven't mentioned the ones who keep souvenirs or mementos, you know, trophies of their crimes."

Cross smiled at her. "Good point, Polly. Some killers keep them, others don't, and trophy-keeping is spread over all the types."

"What about copycat killers?" said Grave.

"Excellent point, sir. Copycats not only seek to copy a crime but to seek approval from the real serial killer, whom they idolize. You'll also find copycats in group killing situations. The lead killer recruits others and trains them in his method of operation."

"So if Clink is involved," said Grave, "perhaps he recruited Gnote or Dough. Is that what you're saying?"

Cross shook his head. "Not necessarily. As far as I know, Clink is very much a loner."

Charlize spoke up. "He is. I can't see him forming a group unless there was some quid pro quo for him to do so."

Cross held up his hands. "I agree with you, but let's not get ahead of ourselves. The first thing we need to do is *do more.*"

"What do you have in mind?" said Grave.

Cross went to the white board and tapped on the name of Wayne John Dough. "We have to find this man and bring him in." He swept his arm close to the white board. "Then all of this should make sense."

Grave hated sitting alone in Morgan's old office. It was like sitting in the man's grave. Every nook and cranny brought back memories of earlier cases and their efforts to solve them, despite the occasional foolish notion of Captain Morgan. But it was what it was. Morgan was sitting in his houseboat, cutting off the tips of his fingers one by one while a search committee labored to find his replacement. Grave could only hope that the committee would avoid Retective Tilda Must entirely.

He glanced through the glass walls that formed Morgan's fishbowl office. Must was sitting at a desk, her head in her hands, glowering at him. If she had had magical powers he would already be a frog. He wondered if he should say something to her, but quickly shook off the thought.

What he needed to do was think of the murders. Cross's presentation had been fine as far as it went. Having him around was going to be a big plus going forward. But they were still in the weeds in terms of solving the case, or cases. Grave knew they had to be connected, but piecing this intricate puzzle together was eluding them.

He checked his watch. Cross and Loblolly should be rolling up to Dough's reported address in just minutes. If Dough was there, they'd bring him in for questioning. If not, they carried a warrant allowing them forced entry into the house. One way or another, they would learn more than they currently knew.

He thought of Polly again and sighed. He was clearly infatuated with her, but he didn't know how to close the deal. What was he thinking, he didn't even know how to *start* the transaction. Women were a mystery to him, and courtship was not among his skills. It was as if he and Polly were playing different games. While he was trying to get to first base, she was enjoying slap shots, hat tricks, and power plays, leaving him standing at home plate with an iced puck. They were like two sports analogies passing in the night.

He sighed again, heavy enough to attract the attention of his partner, Sergeant Barry Blunt, who was sitting all the way across the squad room. Blunt rolled his eyes and went back to work.

Work, thought Grave.

He was about to pick up a stack of incident reports—tourists had a way of getting into trouble when exposed to the delights of Crab Cove—but excited shouts coming from just outside the doors to the station encouraged him to drop the documents and walk out into the squad room. What in the world is going on outside?

The answer came quickly as former Captain Henry Morgan burst into the squad room, carrying a box filled with Captain Morgan Rum tchotchkes. Six very happy Officer Larrys followed him in, trailed by Detective Snoot and the captain's personal drone, Rum, who was brandishing his little cutlass and laughing.

Morgan caught sight of Grave. "I'm back!"

Grave was stunned, then giddy, then ecstatic. "What? How?"

Morgan pointed at Snoot. "All her doing." He pointed the box in the direction of his office. "Come on, I'll fill you in."

51

Loblolly tried to focus on the road as she and the newly minted Detective Alex Cross hovercruised closer and closer to the address they were given for Wayne John Dough. But her thoughts were more on Grave than the road. He should have at least made a move by now. She could see that he liked her, so what was the problem?

"That was a big sigh," said Cross. "What's up?"

She glanced over at him. "Nothing."

He chuckled. "Now that I've had my psychological programming, I know full well that a sigh like that is never about nothing. Come on, out with it. We're partners, right?"

She let out a big breath. "Partners, yes. Priest and confessor, no."

He nodded. "I get it. It's personal."

"Very."

"All right, I won't press you on it. Just know that I'm here for you, if and when you ever need me."

She forced a smile. "Good to know. Thank you, I'll keep that in mind."

"You're welcome."

The hovercruiser hovercruised onward, the two of them maintaining an uncomfortable silence for some minutes, until Loblolly sensed the need to release the pressure by changing to a new topic.

"So," she said, "how do you like being Dr. Alex Cross?"

He seemed surprised by the question. "Really? You really want to know?"

"I do."

"Okay, I feel *odd*."

Loblolly turned and glanced at him, trying to keep her eyes on the road. "Odd in what way."

"Don't laugh, but I feel I was better at being God."

Loblolly snorted. "God? Why?"

"I'm still trying to grasp it, but it's like being God was easier. You know, I was responsible for everything but accountable for nothing. My time was my own. Being God, I could do whatever I liked, without consequences. It was almost, um, relaxing."

"And being Alex Cross?"

He looked down at his clothes. "For one thing, I don't like these clothes. Who dresses like this?"

"Well, obviously, Alex Cross."

"Yes, but on purpose? It's just weird and uptight. You'd think a man so in control of his psychological makeup would choose less restrictive clothing. I mean who wears a suit and tie anymore, am I right?"

"Um, Grave."

"Well, that's perfect for Grave."

"Come on, I think it's kind of cute."

"But I don't want to be cute. And another thing, there's so much pressure to perform. I'm supposed to know the innermost thoughts and motives of the criminal mind."

"But you were programmed to do that. No problem, right. The knowledge is right there at the tip of your circuits."

He scoffed. "Knowledge isn't the point. The point is the pressure to get it right, to track down this killer before he strikes again. God doesn't have to do that. All outcomes are just outcomes to him. Wax on, wax off, it just doesn't matter to him."

"Is that really what's bothering you?"

He hesitated, then said, "Well, I do like God's choice in clothes."

"White and loose-fitting."

"Yes, so comfortable."

She chuckled. "Well, then, maybe you should switch back to being God."

"You think?"

"Sure, why not, but not today. We need your psychological profiling skills right now. And I do mean right now. Look, we're here."

Loblolly slowed the hovercruiser to a stop in front of a boarded up house two blocks off the beach.

Cross was already shaking his head. "This can't be right."

She double-checked the house number. "But according to his student application, this is the place."

"It's a place, all right, but it's all boarded up. Probably wasting our time."

"Maybe, but let's have a look-see anyway."

He shrugged. "Your call."

They got out of the hovercruiser and slowly approached the house.

52

Captain Henry Morgan couldn't believe he'd been out of the office for only a few days. It felt like years had passed by. He took a deep breath—it even *smelled* different.

He set the box down on top of his desk and began taking out the many Captain Morgan Rum logo items, from shot glasses to pocket knives, to caps, to miniature cutlasses, to cigar cutters, to miniature license plates. Each item had a special place on the captain's desk and book shelves, the locations clearly marked by an absence of dust.

He worked quickly, placing item after item, then turned back to his desk and dropped the box to the floor. "There."

Grave, who was sitting in a guest chair, along with Snoot, took *there* as his signal to speak. "So, I heard about the mayor's arrest, but, um, why are you back?"

The captain pointed at Snoot and smiled. "She did it. She did it all."

"Sir, it was nothing," said Snoot.

"Don't be silly. I'd still be out there cutting my fingers if you hadn't pressed the City Council."

Grave turned to Snoot. "Wow."

Snoot shrugged. "It really wasn't such a big deal. Turns out the City Council didn't realize that the captain had been forced out."

"Or that I was closing in on the mayor," said Morgan. "He and the Sons of Irony."

Grave raised an eyebrow. "The Sons? Wow."

"Nothing new. The same old money laundering, but Mayor Change was too bold and careless."

"So you brought in the FBI?" said Grave.

Morgan shrugged. "Had to. All federal crimes. Anyway, the mayor got wind of my investigations—"

"And canned him," said Snoot.

"Well, more like forced retirement, but yes."

Grave smiled at the captain. "It's great to have you back. I'll move my stuff off your desk and get back to mine." He stood. "Then I'll bring you up to speed on the latest developments in the murders."

Morgan held up both hands and waved them in front of himself. "Oh, no you won't. Those cases are yours, start to finish."

Grave pushed back. "But you're the captain, captain."

Morgan laughed. "I am, and it feels good to be back, but as I always say, *never change horses in the middle of a stream*."

Grave frowned, then nodded his head. "All right, but let me tell you, this job—*your* job—is something I hope never to experience again."

The captain scoffed. "From what I've seen and heard, you're doing a fine job, so don't close your mind to the possibility. I'm back now but I won't be here forever."

He looked at Snoot. "I can't thank you enough, Amanda." He looked around the office, beaming. "I love this place, and you gave it back to me."

Snoot smiled. "Great to have you back, sir."

Morgan turned back to Grave. "Now, off with you both. Give a man a little time to drink all this in."

He suddenly looked concerned. "Where's Rum?"

Grave looked out at the squad room. "Looks like he's getting you some coffee, sir."

"Ah," said Morgan. "Ah." He leaned back and rubbed the arms of his chair like he was grooming his favorite horse.

53

After circling the house and peeking in several windows, Cross announced what Loblolly already knew. "We're gonna have to bust in."

"Right," said Loblolly. "I'll get the ram."

"No, wait, I can do this." He walked up to the front door, pushed on it gently in several places, and then kicked it open with an amazingly forceful kick.

"Wow," said Loblolly.

Cross shrugged. "Not much of a challenge for a simdroid. Come on, let's see what we can see."

They walked inside, took out their flashlights, and began assessing the scene. If Dough was living here, it was a bare and spare existence. Not much furniture balanced by a lot of dust. A small coffee table positioned between a recliner and an old-fashioned television held a lone empty pizza box, a used napkin, and an empty bottle of cheap whiskey. All the shades were drawn.

"Living the good life," said Loblolly.

Cross chuckled. "And in the dark. Come on, let's keep moving."

They walked from the living room, through an empty dining room, and into the kitchen. Loblolly began opening cupboards while Cross checked out the old refrigerator-synthesizer.

"The cupboards are mostly bare," said Loblolly. "A few cans of soup and a bag of steak synthesizer powder."

"I don't think I've ever seen a refrigerator-synthesizer this old," said Cross. "Just a few cans of beer and what looks like a vain attempt at a synthesized apple."

"Thus the pizza," said Loblolly.

Cross nodded. "Probably. Perhaps he had more important things on his mind than food."

"Could be. All right, let's check out the bedroom."

They backtracked through the dining room and took a left to the one bedroom in the house. The bed was unmade, one extremely dirty sheet coiled in its center, next to a stained pillow. The drawers to a bureau across from the bed were open.

"Looks like he was leaving," said Loblolly. "Drawers are empty and nothing on top, not even spare change."

Cross scanned the room with his flashlight. "Open closet. No clothes. No suitcase. Looks like we've got a runner."

Loblolly nodded. "Looks like. Let's check out the bathroom." She pointed her flashlight at a door across the room. "I'm guessing that's it."

Cross led the way, then opened the door, which swung open with a loud screech. The smell almost overwhelmed his olfactory sensors. "Oh, my. You may want to let me handle this."

Loblolly held her nose and backed away. "With pleasure."

Cross directed his flashlight to the toilet, which had stopped up and overflowed its bowl. "Just fecal matter." He directed his flashlight to the dirty sink and countertop. "No toothbrush or razor. In fact, nothing at all."

He backed out of the bathroom and shut the door. "That bathroom alone is more than enough to make anyone flee."

"You got that right. Come on, let's see if this house has a basement."

They walked back toward the kitchen. The first door they tried was a broom closet without a broom. "Housekeeping was not his thing," said Loblolly.

"Apparently not," said Cross. He swung his flashlight to another door. "Let's check out this one over here."

They walked over and opened the door. Steps led down to a basement darker than dark. Cross shined his flashlight down the steps. "It's pretty steep. Be careful and stay close."

They walked slowly down the stairs, Cross going first, Loblolly resting her hands on his shoulders to maintain her balance and avoid pitching forward. "I see what you mean."

The basement appeared to be as empty as the rest of the house. There was an old washing machine and dryer in one corner, a furnace in the center, and an old bicycle resting against a far wall, its handlebars bent, presumably from an accident. "Well, he didn't escape on a bicycle," said Cross. He shined his flashlight from wall to wall, finally stopping on a door with three padlocks. "What have we here?"

They moved to the door. "Old combination locks," said Loblolly. "Now what?"

"We go in," said Cross.

"But how?"

Cross handed his flashlight to Loblolly. "Shine the light right on this spot."

Loblolly took the flashlight and pointed it at the door. "Okay, now what? Are you going to do your he-man thing again?"

She didn't have to wait long for an answer. Cross's fist broke through the center of the door, and then he pulled it off its frame.

"Nice," said Loblolly. She handed him back his flashlight.

They walked in, their flashlights scanning the room. There was a blood-covered operating table with restraining straps in the center of the room. A second table up against a far wall contained an array of surgical tools, some clean, some bloody.

"I think we have a winner," said Loblolly.

Cross didn't answer right away. He had moved to another wall, where news clippings and photographs had been pinned. "Indeed we do."

And then he spotted the freezer.

54

Grave and Snoot sat in forced silence as Grave's Austin Healey Sprite roared through town, tourists and locals alike cringing and covering their ears as decibel-defying gospel music rattled windows and shook the leaves off trees.

When they reached the scene and Grave turned off the engine, Snoot removed her hands from her ears and nearly collapsed getting out of the little car. "Oh my god!" she said, rubbing her ears, attempting to restore her hearing. "How in hell can you stand that?"

Grave shrugged. "It's just music." He looked up at the house. Polk was standing on the porch, talking to one of his assistants. The entire perimeter of the house had been roped off with crime scene tape, and a dozen Officer Larrys under the direction of Charlize and Smithers-Watson were methodically surveying the yard, looking for anything that might be of value to solving the crimes. Overhead a score of police drones scanned the entire area. If there was something to be found, they would find it.

Polk spotted him right away. "Up here, Grave."

Grave and Snoot walked up the short flight of steps.

"What have we got?" said Grave.

"Well, hello to you, too," said Polk.

"Sorry, but, um, what have we got?"

Polk puffed out his cheeks. "Well, pretty much a bonanza of DNA evidence."

"Great, do we have any matches?"

"Yes, and probably not much of a surprise to you. We have trace DNA for Ann Aesthesia and our elusive serial killer, Chester Clink."

"So Clink is our killer."

"Not necessarily," said Polk. "There was other DNA evidence, a male, and it's everywhere. Presumably it belongs to Wayne John Dough, if that's even his real name."

Grave nodded at Snoot. "Come on, let's have a look."

"Wait," said Polk. "There's more."

"Oh?"

"A freezer, down in the basement, filled with nonmatching body parts. If this is Dough's work, we have a second serial killer on the loose."

Grave thought of the boat. "And both of them may be long gone by now."

Polk threw up his hands. "Probably, but that's your job, not mine."

Grave nodded. "Right, so are Cross and Loblolly down there?"

"Yes, Cross is working on a theory about the killings."

"Really? What kind of theory?"

Polk shook his head. "You'll have to get that from him. Meanwhile my team will continue searching the area."

"Right," said Grave, turning to Snoot. "Come on, let's see what Cross and Loblolly have found."

Snoot followed him into the house and down the stairs to the basement. Portable lights had been set up to fully illuminate the room. Cross and Loblolly stood facing a wall filled with news clippings and photographs, and didn't see Snoot or Grave when they walked in.

"Cross," said Grave, startling Cross and Loblolly from their intense examination of the wall's contents.

"Captain," said Cross.

"Not any more, Captain Morgan has been reinstated."

"Wow," said Loblolly. "When did that happen?"

"Just a while ago. The mayor's been arrested, and Snoot here convinced the City Council to bring back the captain."

Loblolly turned to Snoot. "Way to go, partner."

Snoot smiled. "It wasn't that difficult. Once they knew the facts about Morgan's forced retirement, it was a no-brainer."

Grave brought them back to the topic at hand. "So, I hear you have a theory, Cross."

Cross nodded. "Still piecing it together, but mostly, yes."

"Care to share?"

Cross pointed to the wall. "It's all right there on the wall, or most of it is."

Grave stepped closer and examined the wall. There were pictures of Ann and Grace—at home, at work, at invisibility training, and walking through the square. "So he stalked them?"

"He did," said Cross, "but that's not all. Look at the clippings."

Grave turned back to the wall. It only took a few seconds to realize their importance. "These are clippings of Clink killings."

Cross nodded. "Yes and not a single unrelated murder. It's all an homage to Chester Clink."

Grave was about to respond, but he saw Polk rushing into the room and stopped. "Jeremy?"

Polk was bent over, trying to catch his breath. Running was not something he did every day. "A body. In a tree. Invisible. Hanging."

The meat hooks and the ropes were clearly visible, but the body was not, save for a pool of blood beneath it. So, after several minutes craning their necks to see what could not be seen, Grave gave the order to cut the body down.

"Polk, have a look," he said. "Anything you can give us."

Polk knelt over the body and ran his gloved hands over what appeared to be the shape of a man. "A man, all right." He motioned to an assistant, who came over and handed Polk the DNA scanner. Polk moved the instrument over the body, then looked at the display. "Matches the dominant DNA inside the house. My guess would be Wayne John Dough."

Cross stepped forward. "I think we'll find that's exactly who it is once we get Rippley Blunt to make him visible again."

Grave sighed. "We've put that girl through a lot, so I'm not going to bring her to the scene. It would just be too much." He turned to Polk. "Take the body and do your thing. I'll get Barry and June to bring her to the morgue."

Polk nodded, started to move away, and then turned back. "I assume I can take the frozen body parts."

Grave nodded. "Yes, of course. If there's a silver lining in any of this, we're going to be closing a lot of missing persons cases up and down the Atlantic seaboard."

"Right," said Polk. "Okay, I'll handle it, but there's going to be extra work for you guys, too. A lot of coordination with multiple jurisdictions."

"Understood," said Grave. He watched as Polk gave a quick final nod and walked back to his team, who were already rolling toward the body with a stretcher and body bag.

Grave turned to Cross and the others. "I know everyone is eager to hear Cross's theory, but let's not do it here." He checked his watch. "We should have a positive ID on the body in the next couple of hours. Let's take a break, grab some lunch, and reconvene back at the station at, say, two. Does that work for you?"

Everyone nodded or grunted affirmation except Cross. "Sir, I'd like to go to the morgue. Be there when the body becomes visible."

Grave nodded. "Of course." He turned to the others. "Okay, then, see you at two."

Everyone started moving away from the scene, including Snoot.

Grave called after her. "Hey, aren't you riding with me?"

Snoot rolled her eyes. "Not on your life."

56

Grave took advantage of the break to head home for lunch. Barry had called ahead so Roderick wouldn't be surprised. Even so, there was no evidence of lunch when Grave climbed the stairs to the kitchen. Roderick was standing in what looked like someone's living room from a bygone era. His lookalike, Peter Lorre, was pointing a small-caliber gun at Humphrey Bogart, who seemed annoyed at the unfriendly gesture.

Roderick noticed Grave and quickly turned off the Surround Vision. "The Maltese Falcon. One of my—I mean his—better roles, don't you think?"

Grave had never thought about it. Not once. "Yes, of course." He looked around the kitchen. "Where's lunch?"

Roderick raised a finger into the air. "Ah, I wasn't sure when you'd show up, so I decided on a cold plate of this and that." He walked to the refrigerator-synthesizer and pulled out a large plate. "Crab, shrimp, caviar, an assortment of greens, and a selection of sauces for dipping."

Grave smiled. "That will do nicely."

"No, it won't," said a familiar voice behind him.

Horace flew across the room and landed on the kitchen table. "Where are the french-fries?"

Roderick groaned. "French-fries, french-fries, it's always french-fries with you."

Grave chuckled. "Well, to be honest, I could use some french-fries as well, and maybe a cheeseburger. These murders have me ravenous."

Roderick rolled his eyes. "The two of you. I don't know what I'm going to do with you. You tell me to have lunch ready but don't say what sort of lunch you want."

"Um, sorry," said Grave.

"I'm not a mind reader, you know."

"Okay, I get it. I'll give you a menu next time."

Roderick sighed and walked over to the refrigerator-synthesizer. "Two orders of french-fries and a cheeseburger, coming up."

Grave sat down at the table, Horace moving to face him on the opposite side of the table.

"You look tired," said Horace.

Grave shrugged. "This captaincy thing, not to mention four murders."

"Four? I thought we were talking about three."

"A new one, possibly a new serial killer named Wayne John Dough."

Horace cackled. "John Doe? Sounds made up."

"It might be. We're still working on that angle. Anyway, we found him hanging from a tree outside his house, on meat hooks."

Horace ruffled his feathers and cringed. "Meat hooks? Eek."

"The guy had a freezer in the basement, full of body parts."

"Yikes."

Grave picked up a fork and poked at the lumps of crab meat on the plate. "Would you like some crab?"

Horace cocked his head at the plate. "Maybe later, after the french-fries." He glanced over at Roderick, who was busy pressing buttons on the synthesizer panel. "If we ever get any."

"I heard that," said Roderick.

"I'm just sayin'," said Horace. He turned back to Grave. "So do you think Clink is involved in this?"

"Almost definitely. First, some of the wounds on the third victim, Cliff Gnote, were an exact match to Clink's Bowie knife. Second, as I told you last night, your pal Arnold dive-bombed the scene of the first murder."

"To warn her."

"We think so, but it's still not clear."

"And how's this Officer Larry working out? Is he still God?"

Grave speared a shrimp and held it up, getting ready to eat it. "No, he's now Alex Cross, a forensic psychologist that Morgan Freeman played in several movies, most notably *Along Came a Spider*."

Horace flapped his wings. "I like spiders, those big ones anyway. Crunchy on the outside, soft and gooey on the inside."

Grave lowered the fork and dropped it on the plate. "Thanks for sharing."

"Sorry." He took a few steps closer to Grave. "So, is there anything I can do to help?"

Grave cocked his head. "Like what?"

"You know, do some reconnaissance maybe."

"Of what?"

Horace shrugged. "Um, Arnold perhaps?"

"But he's now invisible."

"Still, if he's in the area, I know more than a few of his haunts. I can ask around, maybe get a lead on him and that Clink fellow."

Grave considered the offer. "Aren't you worried about the military finding you?"

Horace shook his head. "Not at all. Now that I'm back in Crab Cove, among thousands and thousands of other seagulls—well, you can see how difficult that would be for them."

"So long as you keep your mouth shut."

"Point taken."

Grave sighed. "All right, go for it."

Horace let out a pleased shriek, which almost made Roderick drop the plates of fries and cheeseburgers. "Oh, the two of you. I don't know how much more I can stand."

"Don't worry," said Horace. "I'll be out of your hair momentarily. Our good friend Simon has just deputized me to solve all these murders."

"Whoa, whoa," said Grave. "I never said anything about deputizing you."

"But it's perfect, don't you see? Now the military can't just grab me. I'm a fully deputized police detective."

"Are not."

"Am too."

Roderick rapped his serving tongs down, hard, on the table. "Whatever," he said. "Just eat the damned fries and get out!"

Then he held a hand to his mouth and giggled. "That was my best Peter Lorre, I think."

Grave and Horace just stared at him.

57

Identifying Wayne John Dough as the latest victim took only a few minutes. Rippley knew now what was expected of her and marched directly to the body, laid on her hands, and made him visible. She turned to the others—Cross, Polk, and her mother—and gave them a quick nod. "It's Wayne."

Polk bowed in her direction. "Thank you, young lady. You have been of immense help."

Rippley frowned. "No, not really. I started all of this. If it hadn't been for me and my school, none of this would have happened."

Cross went down on one knee so he could look her in the eye. "This is *not* your fault. Murderers always find a way."

"But I made them *invisible*."

"You made Grace and Ann invisible when they were in trouble and needed your help. You gave them a chance they wouldn't have had otherwise."

She shook her head. "I know you're trying to make me feel better, but remember, I also trained Wayne here. He's one of the killers, isn't he? I know how he looked at them. I should have said something or done something."

Cross sighed. "No, what happened was going to happen. There is nothing that you could have said or done to change the outcome. They were targeted by professional killers who would have found a way, even without the ability to become invisible."

Rippley turned to her mother. "Can we go?"

June looked at Cross, who nodded back. "Yes, honey."

Rippley turned back to Cross and frowned. "Thank you for your kind words, but I know what I did and know now what I must do."

With that, she turned on her heels, grabbed her mother's hand, and tugged her out the door.

Cross watched her go, then turned to Polk. "That's one amazing child."

Polk nodded. "Precocious."

"At a minimum." He nodded at the table and the body of Wayne John Dough. "Let's see what we've got here."

58

Loblolly drummed her fingers on her desk. "Can't wait for this meeting to begin."

Snoot, who was watching the latest press conference on the arrest of Mayor Lester "Les" Change, nodded absently. "Uh-huh."

Loblolly looked at the screen. "Haven't you had enough of that?"

Snoot shook her head. "I don't think I'll ever get enough of it. So glad to see that droid go."

"I never liked him."

"I remember. What puzzles me is how he came to be programmed for criminal activity."

Loblolly snorted. "Probably a standard feature of the Politician Package."

Snoot had to smile. "Yeah, well, whatever." She grabbed the remote and turned the television off.

"Thank you," said Loblolly. She looked at her watch. "Still some time before the meeting."

"Yeah, do you think Cross will come through?"

"I hope so." She cocked her head. "No, I know so. That new programming of his is amazing. It's like he knows what everyone is thinking. What's motivating them. What makes them tick."

Snoot gave Loblolly a long sly look.

"What?" said Loblolly.

"Um, I was just thinking. Maybe you should ask him what gives with Grave. I mean, everyone can see he likes you, so why in hell hasn't he pulled the trigger?"

Loblolly slumped back in her chair. "I don't know and I'm beginning not to care."

Snoot leaned toward her. "Or you could just force the issue, ask him out."

"You think?"

"These are modern times, deary. If he's the man you want, go for him."

Loblolly screwed up her face, then shook her head. "No, well maybe, but I think you're right. I'll talk to Cross first."

The sound of doors being pushed open drew Snoot's attention to the front of the room. Cross and Polk had just come in. "And speaking of whom, here he comes."

"Great," said Loblolly. "Time to get this party started."

Grave wasn't sure how much help Horace would be, but any lead would be welcomed at this point. He thought of the abandoned boat and sighed. Clink, as usual, was probably long gone. And now, with his ability to become invisible at will, he might be able to evade capture forever. And worse, increase the frequency of his killings.

He waved goodbye to Horace from the observation deck of the lighthouse, then took the stairs down to the main level. Red the simcrab was at the tiny console of his data analyzer, his claws punching buttons and twisting dials.

"How's it going, Red?"

Grave's voice startled him. "Damn, Grave, do you have to sneak up on folks?"

"Sorry, I thought you would have heard me."

Red raised his eye stalks. "Well, obviously, I didn't. Now, if you'll excuse me, I have data to process. A schedule is a schedule, and I'm way behind."

Grave frowned. "Behind? That's not like you."

"You think?" He stopped punching buttons, turned to face Grave, and threw up his claws. "It's the damned *turbulence*."

"Oh?"

"My job, as I've tried to explain before, is to collect data on the crab population of the bay. To do that I need to make reliable counts."

"And you can't do that with turbulence."

"Exactly, and it's all because of that damned submarine."

"Wait, what?"

"It just goes back and forth from a cave on the Eastern Shore to a cave on the Western Shore, and every time it does that, it creates turbulence on the sea floor, scattering the crabs and creating complete chaos for me and my count."

Grave had stopped listening at *damned submarine*.

60

Detective Alex Cross wondered whether he should have stayed God. Then he could simply make Grave appear in an instant. As it was, Grave was late, leaving Cross and the others at loose ends. Loblolly and Snoot were at their adjacent desks, talking in whispers. He could see Captain Morgan with his feet up on his desk, sleeping, his drone, Rum, practicing his cutlass skills. Sergeant Barry Blunt was shuffling papers, a frown fixed on his face because of his forced detachment from the case. His drone, Object, sat quietly on Blunt's desk, its rotors still. And Charlize and Smithers-Watson were in a far corner, talking to Retective Tilda Must, who looked beyond upset. Charlize had a hand on her shoulder, trying to offer her some comfort. Her chances at the captaincy had been completely dashed by the arrest of the mayor and the rehiring—or *unretirement*—of Captain Morgan. Cross had no opinion who would make the best captain. He was just too new to the detective corps.

He checked his watch—Grave was now more than twenty minutes late—and then looked up to find Charlize standing right in front of him.

"Grave's late," he said.

"Obviously," said Charlize. "Can't we just get started without him?"

"No. Last time I looked, he was running this show. Besides, we're also missing Polk."

"I thought you had all you needed from Polk."

"As to the killing of Wayne John Dough, yes, but Polk was still working on the various body parts we found in the freezer."

Charlize shook her head. "Well, if I know Jeremy Polk, that kind of investigation could take hours, if not days."

"No, he said it would only take an hour or so, and that *hour* and that *so* passed by about half an hour ago. He should be here." He looked down at his watch again. "Sheesh."

"Well, can I at least tell you how I think everything fits together?"

"I'd really like you to wait on that, so everyone can hear it."

Charlize charged ahead anyway. "It all comes down to a quid pro quo that went wrong, right?"

Cross was about to respond when the doors to the station pushed open. An Officer Larry burst in carrying a badly damaged drone.

"What have we here?" said Cross.

Loblolly answered the question from across the room. "That's my Pine Cone!"

She leaped up from her desk and took the poor drone from Officer Larry. "Where did you find her?"

Officer Larry pointed at the door. "Just outside. A seagull dropped her on the steps."

Loblolly turned to Cross and Charlize. "Do you think it was Clink's seagull, um, Arnold?"

Cross shook his head. "No, that would be too noble a gesture for Chester Clink. If anything, he would have broken up your drone and distributed the parts at sea."

Charlize nodded. "Clink is up to something. But what?"

"I don't care," said Loblolly. "I have my Pine Cone back."

"He looks a little worse for wear," said Snoot, walking up to join them. "Probably needs a look-see by the drone techs."

Loblolly fumbled for the on-switch, found it, and attempted to coax Pine Cone back to life. The drone made a gurgling sound and fell silent. "Well, that's not good."

"Sounds like a power problem," said Snoot. "Come on, there's a hookup in the conference room. Should be fully charged by the end of our meeting." She turned to Cross. "Speaking of which, are we ever going to get started?"

Cross rolled his eyes. "There's a lot to cover, but we can't begin without Grave and Polk."

Snoot checked her watch. "They're way late."

As if on cue, Polk and Grave pushed through the door and walked directly for the conference room. Grave carried Red in one hand and a rolled up map in the other.

"Sorry to be late," said Grave. "Let's get this meeting started. Come on, everyone." He turned to Cross. "Ready?"

Cross smiled. "More than ready, sir. Um, what's with the crab?"

61

Grave walked into the conference room, spread the map out in front of him, and set Red down on top of it. He looked up at the others, who had taken their usual seats around the table. "This is Red. He'll have something important to tell us at the end of this meeting. For now, let's hear what Polk and Cross have come up with." He sat down and nodded at Cross. "You're up."

Cross stood and began pacing back and forth in front of the white board. "We've gone over all this information, so I won't repeat it. What I'll do is take you through each murder, one by one, in the sequence of their occurrence, and identify the murderer. Then, after I've laid it all out, you'll have your opportunity to agree or not."

He paused to scan the table, looking for any disagreement with his proposed approach. Finding none, he continued. "This all started, as Charlize has already figured out, with a quid pro quo between Clink and Wayne John Dough. We'll get to that shortly, but first let's look at the murder of Grace Gnote. The answer is simple: Cliff Gnote. He received invisibility training from Dough for that express purpose, and Dough was more than happy to provide it."

"But Clink didn't approve," said Charlize.

Cross nodded in a way that suggested agreement and annoyance at being interrupted. "Yes, the actions of his seagull, Arnold, support that. Good point, Charlize. Now, let's move on to Ann Aesthesia. She was killed in copycat fashion by Wayne John Dough. He was trying to prove himself to Clink. An homage, if you will." He looked at Charlize. "And here we come to the quid pro quo. Translating from the Latin, this for that. The *this* was Clink's desire to learn how to become invisible. The *that* was Dough's desire to learn from Clink, particularly his ability to kill at will and frustrate the police at every turn."

He paused to look at the team. Everyone was nodding. They were with him on this. "Okay, now we come to the most important piece of the puzzle. A second quid pro quo." He looked at Charlize, whose mouth was open with surprise. Clink agreed to tell Dough everything, but in return—and as part of the training of Dough—he wanted to kill both Grace and Ann himself. To satisfy his own desires and to show Dough how it was done."

He paused and looked around the room. "Are you with me so far?"

Everyone nodded.

"Now we come to the murder of Ann Aesthesia. Dough, who had spent many hours with her in class, had become obsessed with her. So despite his agreement with Clink, he just couldn't resist killing her himself. Which is exactly what happened. He abducted her in the parking lot, drove her to his house and killed her in a way that he thought Clink would approve of."

He paused again, walked over to the white board, and circled Clink's name, tapping the marker on the name for emphasis. "And Clink was not happy. He ordered Dough to return the body to the square—Dough had botched the killing, his knife wounds no better than a copycat amateur."

Loblolly raised her hand. "Why would he do that? Why not just dispose of the body or put it in the freezer?"

"Good question. As we know from our years' long study of Clink, however, we know he's a perfectionist. Even the thought of being connected to the murder was anathema to him. His thought was to have Dough dump the body in the square in an attempt to tie the murder to Cliff Gnote. And if Dough was spotted dumping the body there, so much the better."

He looked at them all again. "Are you with me?"

They were.

"Okay, so while Dough was dumping the body, Clink was progressing from annoyance to rage. When Dough returned, Clink murdered him on the spot and hung him from a tree as a warning to any other killers out there who sought to copy his methods."

"And what about Cliff Gnote?" said Snoot.

"Ah, the final act. Clink had two reasons for killing Cliff. First, Clink had wanted to kill the man's wife, and second, Cliff was a potential threat. He knew about the deal and Clink's involvement. He simply had to go, he was a loose end, and Clink dispatched him with his Bowie knife, using the same techniques he used on all his other victims."

Grave rose from his chair and stood next to Cross. "And then he made his getaway on Cliff's boat, abandoning it in favor of his submarine." He turned to Cross. "Thank you for your analysis. I think it is spot on." He turned back to the others. "Now all we have to do is capture Clink."

Snoot chuckled sardonically. "As if. He's gone. We all know he's gone."

"Not necessarily," said Grave, turning to Red. "My friend here, Red, is a simscientist whose job is to study crab populations in the Chesapeake Bay. And in those studies, he's had occasion to see said submarine operating between two caves, one on the Eastern Shore and one on the Western Shore."

He nodded at Red, who walked to the center of the map. "Thank you for hearing me out. As elusive as you claim this Clink to be, I think you'll find him." He skittered sideways and tapped at a point on the Eastern Shore. "Here." Then he skittered to the Western Shore. "Or here."

Everyone was wide-eyed, particularly Snoot. "Then let's go get the bastard."

Grave nodded. "The Coast Guard is doing that right now, as we speak. We should have him momentarily."

Grave was about to say more, but Pine Cone suddenly pulled away from the charging station and wobbled to the center of the table, rotating to face everyone in turn. And then he spoke. "Interesting information, but I'm afraid you won't find me at either location."

Charlize recognized the voice immediately. "Clink?"

His laugh was chilling. "Yes, Charlize, yes."

62

Everyone stared in amazement at Pine Cone, who had apparently been taken over by serial killer Chester Clink. He stared back, then chuckled. "I see I've startled you. All well and good. Having the police on their heels is always a good thing—for me."

Grave was the first to find voice, although he could only manage one word. "How?"

"Come now, Grave, taking over a drone is child's play. You're asking the wrong questions."

"And what would be the right questions?" said Cross.

Clink rotated slightly to take in Cross. "You were an Officer Larry once, were you not?"

Cross nodded.

"I remember seeing you in the town square just after the murders. And now look at you, a right *detective*." He spit out the word as if it tasted bad.

"And a forensic psychologist in the bargain," said Cross.

Clink laughed. "I wouldn't call your analysis particularly *forensic*. In fact, I'd call it embarrassing."

Cross cocked his head. "Oh, in what way?"

"No, I'm not here to train you. Let me just tell you what you had right. I think upon reflection you'll figure the rest out."

"I'm all ears."

"What you got right was the quid pro quo, or rather the quid pro quo pro quid." He rotated to face Charlize. "I think you were the first to realize it, were you not."

Charlize nodded, then shook her head. "We both figured it out at about the same time."

"Tch, tch, tch, you are much too modest, Charlize. Why, I bet you would have solved this case in a nonce if you'd been in charge. You know, I fear you the most, what with all your Sherlock Holmes programming. Nothing escapes you, even the smallest details."

Charlize just glared at him.

"Nothing to say, then? Pity, I would have far preferred your analysis of me and the murders. Perhaps you can train your friend here how it's done."

Grave tried to turn the conversation in another direction. "If this is your victory lap, I think we've had enough. But if you'd like to help, I have a few questions for you."

Clink's laugh was loud and long. "Oh, my, me answer *your* questions? Now why would I do that?"

"Because they're about Wayne John Dough."

Clink grew serious. "Oh, him."

"Yes, him."

"All right, but we'll need Polk here to do that."

Polk spoke up. "I'm over here."

Clink rotated in the direction of the voice. "Ah, there you are. I must say, you are much shorter than I imagined."

Polk turned red. "Why you . . ."

"Now, now, no offense intended."

"Get on with it," said Grave. "Why do you need Polk?"

Clink turned to Grave. "One question of me requires several from Polk." He turned back to Polk. "Tell me, when you catalogued the body parts in the freezer, did you find a head?"

Polk nodded. "Yes, one head, an older woman, badly decomposed."

"That would be his mother's head. Dug up at the beginning. Now, did you find two arms?"

"Yes, but from different victims, both women."

"Yes, yes, I think you'll find all the body parts are from women. Now, did you find two hands, a torso, and two legs?"

"Again, yes, yes, and yes."

"But when it came to feet, you were two short." He laughed. "And I meant that as two, T-W-O, not T-O-O."

"That's right, no feet."

Clink sighed. "Wayne wanted the feet of Grace and Ann."

"And why's that?" said Grave.

Clink chuckled. "Don't be a dull boy. He needed them to finish his creation. The mother he always wanted but never had. He had killed her, you see, at age eleven."

"I still don't understand."

Cross interrupted. "I think I see. It was all about guilt."

Clink waggled in the air. "Yes, perhaps there is some hope for you yet, sir."

"Killing his mother rid him of his abuser, but the guilt became overwhelming."

"Yes," said Clink, "so he decided to build a new mother, one better than the original."

"But he kept her head?" said Grave. "I don't get it."

Cross nodded. "Yes, he had to keep her head so she could see his creation, his improvement on every part of her. As a way to remove his guilt while shaming her."

"My, my," said Clink. "The nail has received your hit."

"Okay," said Grave. "He wanted Grace's and Ann's feet, but he didn't get them."

"Because of me. That wasn't part of the quid pro quo pro quid. The women were to be mine, and dismemberment is anathema to me, as I'm sure Charlize here has already figured out."

Charlize nodded. "You like clean kills. Many wounds, but none meant to disfigure, let alone dismember. Then you stage the bodies, making them look almost alive. That's important to you, to show how fine the barrier is between life and death."

Clink turned to Grave. "Oh, how I love this simdroid. She sees me in ways your Officer Larry doesn't." He turned back to Charlize. "Well done, Charlize. I love a worthy adversary."

Charlize leveled her gaze on him. "We'll get you, you know."

Clink chuckled again. "Maybe, but you'd better act fast. I've already selected my next victim." He spun quickly and moved to face Loblolly. "You left your bedroom lights on again this morning, my dear." And with that, the drone dropped to the table, silent and motionless.

Clink—and the air—had gone out of the room.

Epílogue

Grave took a sip of Duct Tape Chardonnay and sighed, knowing it wouldn't fix anything. News from the Coast Guard had come quickly — both caves had been abandoned, and there was no sign of Clink or his submarine. Grave and his team had closed two murder cases, true, but the two attributed to Chester Clink remained open and would probably stay open for months or possibly years. They had never had any luck catching Clink when he was visible, and now that he could become invisible at will, the chances of catching him were slim to none.

He sighed again, this one more nuanced as he reflected on Polly Loblolly. Her life had been threatened and he had neither said nor done anything to indicate his concern, which was real and deep. He should go to her house now, tell her how he felt about her, and take his chances that she had similar feelings. But did she? Cross thought so, and the Reverend Bendigo Bottoms had said much the same thing when Grave had visited him three days after the disastrous meeting where Polly's life had been threatened.

He had gone to the cemetery that day to visit Victoria and see if she had learned anything more from the ghosts of Grace and Ann. Yes, Grave knew now who had killed them, but any additional information from the victims would have been welcome. Perhaps they could shed some light on Chester Clink or even their failed plan to save themselves.

Victoria had just shaken her head. "They just won't talk about it," she had said. "They *do* bicker a bit about their plan, though. Grace keeps saying it should have worked."

Grave had thanked her for trying. "You've been very helpful, as usual, but if you have a chance to press them further, I'd really like to know the details of their plan."

"Will do."

He had started to leave, then had turned back. "Oh, I don't suppose you've heard from Cliff Gnote or Wayne John Dough."

"No, of course not, Simon. They're on an express train to a less friendly place."

"Oh, right."

He had given her a little wave goodbye and had walked to the grave of the reverend, who had then provided the same advice as Cross.

"Love is like a chocolate donut, right?"

"Yes, you've explained that before."

"And Polly is the sprinkles, right?"

"Yes, I guess, but I don't know whether she thinks I'm a chocolate donut, let alone even so much as a single sprinkle."

"Simon, Simon, what am I going to do with you? Go to her, talk to her, let her know how you feel. What's the worst that could happen?"

"I don't know. Maybe she'll think I'm a plain cake donut."

The reverend had rolled his eyes at that, and then had changed the subject. "Speaking of plain cake donuts, what are you going to do to get rid of the chatbot of me?"

Grave had completely forgotten about his promise to help remove the chatbot from the gravesite. "Let me talk to the cemetery director. Perhaps we can come to some accommodation."

"I hope so. And if not, bring a sledgehammer the next time you come. This is getting ridiculous."

Grave and the director had indeed come up with an accommodation, a quid pro quo.

"Take it," the director had said. "We've had so many complaints about it and now two young women have filed a complaint with the police, saying the faux reverend harassed them, made lude comments."

"So you want me to quash the complaint?"

"If you could."

They had shaken hands, and the director had helped Grave load the chatbot of the reverend into the passenger seat of the Sprite.

The faux reverend had complained at first, but once Grave started up the Sprite and the deafening gospel music began, the faux reverend had slumped back in his seat, a serene smile on his face.

When they had arrived back at the lighthouse, the faux reverend had begged to remain in the car, which he called paradise. Grave had relented, at least until he could think of a better home for him.

He had left him in the car and now stood on the observatory platform of the lighthouse.

He took another sip of wine. Even at the top of the lighthouse, he could hear the faux reverend shouting out a sermon. "By his donuts ye shall know him!"

***

Rippley Blunt knocked lightly on Penelope Goodlove's bedroom door, which swung open almost immediately.

"Oh, it's you," said Penelope. "What can I do for you?"

Rippley stepped into the room, which looked more like an office than a bedroom. "Um, I like what you've done here."

Penelope put her hands on her hips. "Thank you. Not much, but it will have to do until I can afford office space."

Rippley turned slowly in a circle, trying to take it all in. A small desk with a computer sat against one wall. Penelope's bed, which was shaped like a racing car, sat against another wall, covered in teddy bears. A third wall contained a floor-to-ceiling whiteboard filled with notes and lists with connecting arrows in black and red marker. And the fourth wall contained the door to the room, which was also covered in news clippings, photographs, and post-it notes. There was only one word that came to Rippley's mind. "Wow."

Penelope seemed pleased. "This is where the magic happens."

"Yeah, I saw the sign on the door."

"I struggled with the name, but *Penelope Goodlove's Invisible Detective Agency* seemed to be just right."

Rippley nodded. "Well, I'd like to talk to you about that."

"Oh? What do you mean?"

"I'd like to partner with you."

Penelope seemed surprised. "But what about your school?"

"I'm closing it, probably forever."

Penelope nodded. "The murders."

"Yes."

Penelope frowned. "I'm not sure I need a partner."

"Come on, two heads are better than one. We could solve cases faster, take on more cases, move to a *real* office."

Penelope nodded. "Might work, but I can't pay you, at least not yet."

"So, am I in?"

Penelope beamed at her. "Yes!"

Rippley reached out and gave her a hug. "We'll be a great team."

"I know. Now, let me go over our current cases."

"No, wait, can we discuss the name?"

Penelope frowned. "But I like the name. What, do you want something boring like Goodlove and Blunt Investigations?"

Rippley was already laughing. "No, no way. But hear me out. The current name is okay, but I don't think it should contain the word invisibility. That just gives away our ace up the sleeve and makes us sound like snoops."

Penelope wrinkled her brow. "We're not snoops."

"No, of course not."

"Then what name do you suggest."

"Something more evocative and easy to remember."

Penelope shrugged. "Well, what?"

Rippley glanced at Penelope's birthmark. "How about Red Owl Investigations?"

Penelope's hand shot up to cover her birthmark. "No!"

Rippley put a hand on her shoulder. "I know you're sensitive about it, but you shouldn't be. It's a wonderful owl, and you should own it, girl."

Penelope dropped her hand and sighed. "Maybe. Let me think about it."

"Sure, no rush."

Penelope smiled at her and pointed at the whiteboard. "Let's get to it. We have three cases. That espionage thing involving the chess players—I'll continue to work on that with the FBI. Then there's a problem at the Warren place—Mrs. Warren says someone is stealing her favorite roses. And finally, there's the case I'd like you to take on—just for starters."

"Okay, what is it?"

"A missing cat named Mr. Peebles."

Rippley seemed crestfallen. "Oh."

"Oh, no, don't think it's less of a case. I mean, espionage is hard, admittedly, but cats are harder. Much harder."

***

The discovery of a new Clink victim three days later, on a beach two hundred miles away, had given Loblolly enough courage to venture out to dinner at Le Crabe Bleu with Detective Snoot. Her bodyguards, four Officer Larrys, kept vigilance a few tables away as ten police surveillance drones equipped with heat-sensing cameras hovered overhead.

"So," said Snoot, "do you think it was an empty threat, this Clink thing?"

Loblolly sighed. "I hope so, but I honestly don't know. Captain Morgan wants to keep protection in place, at least for a few more weeks."

"Sounds right." Snoot looked up at the drones. "So, have you given any thought to a new drone?"

Loblolly brightened. "Yes, I've been looking at one of those new mirrored drones, the ones that sparkle in the sunlight."

Snoot gave her a disapproving smirk. "Do you really want that much attention? When Clink finds out, and he will, you'll be pretty easy to find." She took a sip of wine. "No, what you need is a stealthy drone like my Midnight."

Loblolly looked up. Midnight was doing loops around the police drones. "Midnight is fine for you. Goes with your penchant for black, um, *everything*."

"Well, whatever you get, get one that can't be taken over by Clink.

That whole episode in the conference room just blew my mind."

Loblolly cringed. "It was awful."

Snoot took another sip of wine and glanced over at the Officer Larrys, who were looking in all directions, searching for any hint of Chester Clink. "Cross was good, though, wasn't he?" She raised her glass to take another sip.

Loblolly rolled her eyes. "Yes, but now he's not sure he wants to be Cross anymore."

Snoot almost spit out her wine. "Oh, my god, don't tell me he wants to be God again."

Loblolly shrugged. "He was very secretive, but I sensed he was excited about the possibility of something new. A whole new direction."

"Speaking of which," said Snoot. "Any word from Grave?"

Loblolly rolled her eyes even harder. "Not a peep since I went under protection. I tell you, Amanda, I'm done with him."

Snoot cocked her head. "Yeah, right."

"No, I'm serious this time. He's just so, so *frustrating*."

"You should ask Cross about him."

Loblolly sighed. "I did."

"So what did he say?"

"He said I should take the first step, that Grave was one of those men who had few recognizable social skills. He said it was just not in Grave's makeup to make the first move."

Snoot nodded. "Sounds about right to me. So why not follow the advice?"

Loblolly puffed out a breath. "Maybe, I don't know." She looked at the Officer Larrys and then up at the drones. "Certainly not with all these guys around."

"I hear you. But don't give up."

Loblolly nodded absently, picked up her glass of Duct Tape Chardonnay, "the wine that can fix anything," and took a sip. *Maybe it can*, she thought. *But probably not.*

Snoot suddenly started laughing.

"What?" said Loblolly.

Snoot pointed to the outdoor entrance to the restaurant. A man resembling Morgan Freeman was walking in. He was dressed in a three-piece white suit with a black string tie, and carried a gold-topped cane. His hair was pure white and long and curly.

"Oh, my god, he didn't," said Loblolly.

"What?"

She didn't have time to answer. The man was standing next to their table now, smiling down at them.

Loblolly could only shake her head. "Oh, Huckleberry."

Note From The Author

Word-of-mouth is crucial for any author to succeed. If you enjoyed *Simon Grave and the School of Casual Invisibility*, please leave a review online—anywhere you are able. Even if it's just a sentence or two. It would make all the difference and would be very much appreciated.

Thanks!
Len

About the Author

Len Boswell is the author of eleven additional books, including mysteries, fantasies, memoirs, and other nonfiction works. He lives in the mountains of West Virginia with his wife, Ruth, and their two dogs, Shadow and Cinder.

Other books by Len Boswell

Simon Grave Mysteries:
A Grave Misunderstanding
Simon Grave and the Curious Incident of the Cat in the Daytime
Simon Grave and the Drone of the Basque Orvilles
Simon Grave and the Sons of Irony

Other Mysteries:
Flicker: A Paranormal Mystery
Skeleton: A Bare Bones Mystery

Memoirs:
Santa Takes a Tumble
Unboxing Raymond

Nonfiction:
The Leadership Secrets of Squirrels
Stick Figures: The Life and Art of Len Boswell

Fantasies:
The Cave of the Six Arrows

We hope you enjoyed reading this title from:

www.blackrosewriting.com

Subscribe to our mailing list – *The Rosevine* – and receive **FREE** books, daily deals, and stay current with news about upcoming releases and our hottest authors.
Scan the QR code below to sign up.

Already a subscriber? Please accept a sincere thank you for being a fan of Black Rose Writing authors.

View other Black Rose Writing titles at
www.blackrosewriting.com/books and use promo code
PRINT to receive a **20% discount** when purchasing.